Other books

Fiction
Just an Odd Job Girl
Flights of Fancy
Tales From the Garden
What's in a Name? – Volume I
What's in a Name? – Volume II

Non-fiction
Size Matters … Especially if you weigh 330 lbs!
Forget the Viagra … Pass Me a Carrot!
Just Food For Health
Turning Back the Clock
Media Training – The Manual

Books are all available via Amazon.
See the Author's Page:

https://www.amazon.com/Sally-Cronin/e/B0096REZM2

WHAT'S IN A NAME?

Stories of life and romance
Volumes 1 & 2 Combined

SALLY CRONIN

Moyhill Publishing

© Copyright 2017 Sally Cronin.

All rights reserved. This book, or any portion thereof, may not be reproduced or used in any manner whatsoever without the express written permission of the author except for the use of brief quotations in a book review.
The moral right of the author has been asserted.

Print Edition 2017
ISBN 9781905597796.

Printing History:
Volume I previously published in eBook format 2017
Kindle: ASIN: B01N6Y8BK1.
EPUB ISBN 9781905597734.

Volume II previously in eBook format 2017
Kindle: ASIN B0748MLZ1W.
EPUB: ISBN 9781905597789.

A CIP catalogue record for this book is available from the British Library.

Designed & typeset by *Moyhill* Publishing.

Printed and bound in Great Britain by
Marston Book Services Ltd, Oxfordshire

The papers used in this book were produced in an environmentally friendly way from sustainable forests.

Moyhill Publishing,
1965 Davenport House, 261 Bolton Rd,
Bury, Gtr. Manchester BL8 2NZ UK.

Dedication

To Geoff Cronin a master storyteller 1923–2017

Contents

Volume I

ANNE	5
ALEXANDER	8
BEATRIX	13
BRIAN	17
CELIA	20
CLIVE	27
DIANA	33
DAVID	38
ELAINE	43
ERIC	47
FIONNUALA	52
FRANCIS	56
GRACE	61
GEORGE	67
HANNAH	71
HECTOR	76
ISOBEL	82
IFAN	87
JANE	92
JACK	98

Volume II

KENNETH	105
LILY	110
MARTHA	113
NORMAN	119
OWEN	125

Contents

PATRICK 127
QUEENIE 133
ROSEMARY 141
SONIA 146
THERESA 152
USHER 154
VANESSA 158
WALTER 162
XENIA 167
YVES 170
ZOE 176

Bonus Story
The Village Square 185

Acknowledgements 194
About the Author 195
Your feedback would be appreciated 196

Volume I

About Volume I

There are names that have been passed down through thousands of years which have powerful and deep-rooted meanings to their bearers. Other names have been adopted from other languages, cultures and from the big screen. They all have one thing in common. They are with us from birth until the grave and they are how we are known to everyone that we meet.

There are classical names such as Adam, David and Sarah that will grace millions of babies in the future. There are also names that parents have invented or borrowed from places or events in their lives which may last just one lifetime or may become the classic names of tomorrow.

Whatever the name there is always a story behind it. In this first volume of "***What's in a Name***", twenty men and women face danger, love, loss, romance, fear, revenge and rebirth as they move through their lives.

Anne changes her name because of associations with her childhood, Brian carries the mark of ancient man, Jane discovers that her life is about to take a very different direction, and what is Isobel's secret?

ANNE

Anne Fitzgerald was described by her rather aloof mother, to all who would listen, as a plain child. Rather a solemn looking baby, she grew into a chubby toddler with fine straight hair that was tucked behind slightly protruding ears.

Her father, who had adored his daughter from the first time he had held her, adopted a different opinion. He had looked into her blue and slightly unfocused eyes and in that moment was lost. The fact that Anne was to be the only child, and had such a warm and close relationship with her father, did not help the bond with her mother.

Daphne Smith came from a long line of elegant women who were accustomed to standing out from the crowd by the artful use of expensive clothes and exquisite accessories. A name for her yet unborn daughter had been chosen as a tribute to Daphne's exceedingly regal looking grandmother and other generations before her.

However, as Anne developed into a gangly teenager, her mother was quite pleased that dear Grandmamma was no longer around to join her in her critical opinion of her awkward looking offspring.

Despite her mother's disappointment, Anne developed a wonderfully sunny nature and smile with a generous personality. Everyone she met adored her. Much to her mother's surprise, when Anne was in her early 20s, a young and dashing officer in the cavalry proposed to her daughter and was accepted. She was equally surprised that her daughter looked reasonably attractive as she walked down the aisle on the arm of her very proud father. Daphne felt a slight twinge of regret that perhaps she had been a little hasty in her opinion of Anne's attributes and thought that even her grandmother might have approved.

She was however slightly taken aback that the bridegroom referred to his new wife in his wedding speech as Annie, and would continue to do so from that moment on. She was even more annoyed that her own seemingly oblivious husband adopted this common nickname for his daughter too. She felt it was a direct insult to her illustrious ancestors who had proudly borne the name Anne.

Over the years, Annie became a mother to three sons and finally a long awaited daughter. Daphne had been an attentive grandmother as far as dispensing gifts on birthdays and Christmas as well as advice on the upbringing of children. Annie was always gracious and would politely listen to her mother but would glance frequently out into the garden where her father would be playing boisterously with her young sons.

With the birth of a granddaughter, Daphne eagerly awaited the news that the surprisingly beautiful little girl would be named after her. She was astonished when Annie and her husband announced that their daughter would be named Davina a name that celebrated her status as *'beloved'*.

Daphne was far too polite to confront her daughter and her husband but made sure that she made her displeasure known to her seemingly oblivious husband.

He listened for several minutes to the angry words that flowed from his wife's mouth. Apart from the matter of not being honoured in the naming of her granddaughter, there was also the unresolved issue of the over familiar use of 'Annie' in relation to her daughter.

What's in a Name?

'My dear,' her husband raised a calming hand. 'Your daughter associated her given name with your constant disapproval and asked to be known as Annie instead. The reason that she chose the name Davina for her daughter was to let her know that she was much wanted and beloved by her mother, something that she never felt herself.

Daphne sat in shocked silence at this revelation. Her husband's hand closed over hers and squeezed it gently.

'It's not too late my dear,' he looked into his wife's tear-filled eyes.

At the christening of Davina, her grandmother stood slightly away from the happy family group. Tentatively she edged closer to her daughter's side and looked down at the smiling baby in her arms.

'She is very beautiful Annie,' she touched her daughter's arm gently. 'She has your eyes,' she paused for a moment. 'I promise to try and be a better grandmother to her than I was a mother to you.'

Annie smiled back at her mother and thirty years later than nature had intended; the bond between mother and daughter was formed.

ALEXANDER

When Joyce Briggs was sixteen years old, her boyfriend at the time Ernie Winterbottom, took her to the cinema to see the latest epic to hit the silver screen which was *Alexander the Great* with Richard Burton. His aim was twofold. To impress the curvy Joyce with his intellectual prowess by choosing a film that was a bit la-di-dah, and to get her into the back seats of the cinema for a bit of you-know-what!

What Ernie did not take into account was that Joyce was besotted with Richard Burton. The sight of him in his armour as the great Alexander, not to mention his bare knees, had her more of a quiver than the prospect of a kiss and a cuddle with a spotty Herbert of a lad. In fact she barely acknowledged Ernie's presence throughout the action packed two hours and twenty-three minutes. Not only did he not get to snuggle against her ample proportions in the back seat, she talked non-stop all the way home on the top of the bus despite his best efforts to silence her with desperate kisses.

Finally, they arrived at the door of the flat that she shared with her widowed mum and he was just about to turn away and wend his lonely way home when she fluttered her eyelashes at him.

'Me mum's away at my gran's for the night,' she puckered her lips at him suggestively.

'Do you fancy coming in for a cuppa?' Thankful that the evening had not been entirely wasted, Ernie was in the flat as quick as a ferret up a drainpipe.

What's in a Name?

Nine months later to the night, Joyce Winterbottom welcomed her son into the world and announced to the rather reluctant and bemused young father, that he would be called Alexander Richard Winterbottom.

Over the following years Alex, as he liked to be called, often contemplated the fact that he was not living up to his mum's lofty expectations of his illustrious name.

Those few friends that he had at his first school shortened Alex even further to Al; but it was his surname that was his main cross to bear. He was physically rather puny and the resident school bullies referred to him as Frosty Bum as they nicked his lunch money.

At home it was a different story as Joyce regaled him with the legendary tales of his namesake she had discovered in a book from the library. To be kind to his mum; Alex did his very best to look enthusiastic. Even at an early age, he had a sneaky feeling that he could not compete with the legend of the great man, who conquered half the bleeding world before breakfast over 2,000 years previously.

His dad had done a bunk when Alex was three years old and Joyce had lavished all her attention on her beloved Alexander/Burton substitute. Times were hard but after a while she met a plumber called Percy Shufflebottom when he came to fix a leaky pipe.

After a few months of courtship they had set up home in his semi-detached house with the now five year old Alex in tow. Percy was a kind and considerate man and had been a good partner to his mum and step-dad to Alex. When Joyce eventually managed to get a divorce from the elusive Ernie, it left the couple free to tie the knot in the local registry office. At the time, Alex was offered the opportunity to change his name from Winterbottom to Shufflebottom. At eleven years old, Alex knew that moving into secondary

What's in a Name?

school with his current surname would be tough enough, so declined the offer.

Five years later and Alex had grown to a decent height but was still on the runty side. However, he had excelled at sports including long-distance running and football. He was not a duffer but preferred the physical activities rather than sitting in a classroom.

After consultation with the headmaster and his mum when he was sixteen, it was decided that he would get an apprenticeship with a local garage.

So here he was aged twenty and sitting in his pride and joy, a rebuilt Morris Minor, wondering if he would ever get the grease stains from under his fingernails. The rain was pelting down the windscreen and the inside of the car had fogged up. He and his mate Stan had been out to the pub and had fancied some chips and curry sauce on the way home. It would stink up the car but to be fair he was not really bothered. In fact he found he was not particularly bothered about anything these days. He worked hard; lived in a bedsit a few streets from the garage and went round to his mum's on a Sunday for a good feed. But if he was being honest; essentially he just existed.

He wiped the inside of the windscreen with a cloth and looked over at the chippie to see what was holding Stan up. He couldn't see clearly because of the pouring rain and the dim street lighting so he got out of the car, locking the door behind him. He joined the back of the queue which stretched out the door of the cafe and several feet up the pavement. People huddled under their umbrellas and Alex tried to see around them to find out where Stan was in the line. As he did so his eyes were drawn to a large poster in the office window next to him.

What's in a Name?

∽∾

It was December of 1982 and Joyce and Percy waited anxiously in their immaculate living room. Only used for special occasions; it was decorated with the Christmas tree that Percy had picked up at the market and streamers stretched across from each corner of the room. Percy clasped one of his wife's hands as the other fingered her string of pearls around her plump neck.

'Don't worry love, he will be here soon,' he soothed his nervous wife. The clock on the mantelpiece chimed and they both looked across at it for the tenth time in the last hour.

Finally, they heard a car draw up outside and voices talking in the street. Joyce heaved herself out of her chair and pushed past Percy to get into the hall… She tentatively released the catch on the lock and opened the door to face the visitor standing there.

She had not seen her son for two years and she looked at him in wonder. He had filled out a great deal since joining the Royal Navy six years before. He looked so impressive in his new Petty Officer uniform with his cap tucked under his arm. She put her hand to her mouth and then launched herself at him sobbing as he put his strong arms around her.

Behind them Percy looked on fondly. Alexander might not be his son by birth but he was bloody proud all the same. They had waited for days to find out if the lad was safe. Like the parents of those on both sides of the short conflict; they had been glued to the news on the television every night. Huddled on the sofa together, they watched anxiously as naval and land battles had been fought so far away in the Falklands. It had been absolutely terrifying when Alex's ship had been hit several times in an air attack.

What's in a Name?

They were finally told that the lad had been slightly wounded but would be on his way home on leave in time for Christmas. Tears filled Alex's eyes as the two people he loved most in the world each took a hand and led him into the festively decorated living-room. For a moment or two he stood looking around at the streamers and welcoming banners.

Joyce smoothed her hand over her son's gold braid on the sleeve of his uniform and looked up at his handsome face.

She laughed delightedly. 'Well I never love; you look just like Richard Burton…'

BEATRIX

Beatrix De Carlo took her final bow before the audience that filled the theatre to capacity. There had been four curtain calls; as those who had watched her last performance of this critically acclaimed production, showed their appreciation and adoration.

Beatrix remained in character, gently smiling and waving her arm regally at both cast members and audience in turn. Her silver hair shone in the stage lighting and the fake diamonds around her neck sparkled as if to deny their false nature.

Finally, the curtain came down for the last time and members of the cast rushed forward to clasp her hands and utter niceties to her. One after another they politely offered their thanks before heading off to embrace their fellow cast members.

Beatrix could hear them making arrangements to meet up for drinks in the pub around the corner.

'So privileged to have worked with you Miss De Carlo,' whispered the leading man whose breath smelt of mints. She smiled graciously and disengaged herself from his sweaty hands.

'You too Gerald and please give my regards to your lovely wife.' Discouraged, the elderly actor turned and sauntered across the stage intent on joining the younger generation for last orders.

She glided away through the stage crew as they cleared the set and made her way to her dressing room.

What's in a Name?

She closed the door behind her and looked at the cluttered space. Two costume changes lay untidily across the sofa and armchair and instead of the usual welcoming tray of sparkling mineral water and chocolate digestive biscuits, there was a dirty coffee mug containing bitter dregs. She leaned back against the door and closed her eyes wearily. How she missed Mabel.

The theatre management had offered the services of one of their experienced dressers for this last performance but that would have been unacceptable. Mabel was the only person who knew exactly what Beatrix needed and had been by her side for the last fifteen years without missing a single performance. She moved towards the dressing table and sat on the velour stool and looked at herself in the mirror.

Removing her bouffant silver wig, she placed it carefully on the foam model head beside her. She then began the painstaking task of removing the make-up that had transformed her into a seventy year old dowager queen. Finally she was bare faced and viewed her reflection. Having removed one face she must now apply another.

As she slipped her arms into her leather coat and patted her platinum blonde hair into place there was a knock on the door.

'Miss De Carlo, it's Jack Smith, can I come in for a moment?'

Beatrix went across and opened the door for the theatre director and smiled at him.

'Hello Jack,' she laid a hand on his arm. 'I hope you were happy with the final performance this evening?'

He stepped into the dressing room and took in its untidy appearance.

'Sorry to hear about Mabel,' he perched on the back of the armchair. 'Spraining her ankle like that was a great shame but I'm sure she will be back on her feet again very soon.'

Seeing that Beatrix was ready to leave, Jack escorted her to the stage door where she signed out for the last time. She slipped Tony the porter an envelope and he winked back at her in thanks. Leaving the two men behind, she walked into the cold night air and slipped into the back seat of the waiting taxi.

For a moment Jack stood with his hands in his trouser pockets before turning to Tony. 'She really is an amazing woman isn't she,' He paused for a moment and shook his head. 'It is hard to believe that she has stayed at the top of her game for the last forty years.' Tony nodded his head in silent agreement as he slipped the envelope into his pocket.

The taxi driver opened the back door of his cab and assisted the elegant middle aged woman onto the slick pavement. She paid the fare and tipped him generously with a gracious smile. She let herself into the luxury mews cottage where she had lived for the last seventeen years. Carefully she closed the door behind her and let out a sigh of relief.

She could see that there was a light still on in the living-room and she popped her head in and viewed the occupant.

Hi mum,' she smiled at the woman with her foot up on a stool in front of her armchair. 'Can I get you anything before I get out of this clobber?

'No Brenda love, clean that muck off your face and get into your PJs,' she smiled at her daughter mischievously. 'I want to hear all about the last night, I was so gutted to have missed it.'

Ten minutes later her daughter sat on the sofa with her bare feet up on the coffee table. Her auburn hair in a short bob framed her youthful face and she held the cup of hot chocolate between her clasped fingers.

What's in a Name?

The two generations of the acting legend known as Beatrix De Carlo then shared the glory of the latest triumphant performance.

BRIAN

The firelight from the hearth flickered across the stampeding beasts on the wall of the cave. The clan leader Brynyar lay on the animal pelts and tried to gather his thoughts through the pain. He was old at over forty winters and his bones ached with arthritis.

The gash in his side from the bison during the final hunt of the summer had not healed well, and despite the wound being packed with herbs by the medicine woman, it hurt like hell.

His time was near and he was afraid. Not for what was to come, as that was part of the cycle of life. What really worried him was the future of his clan in the changing world around them. Even in his lifetime, he had witnessed the gradual warming of the sun and the melting of ice caps to the north, and this had resulted in massive migrations of the animals they relied on for their food and so much of their daily needs.

The clan would have to move from their ancestral winter caves here in the fertile valley and move with the herds to find a new home. He knew that he would be unable to travel with them and although he trusted his eldest son of his hearth he knew what a huge undertaking it would be.

Brynyar rubbed the back of his hand where a birthmark in the form of an arrow darkened its weathered skin. Each one of his sons carried the same blemish and it was right that they do so. They were the fleetest and most successful of the clans and had a reputation as the finest hunters in the valley. They were also accomplished craftsmen working with flint and bone to produce their much admired weapons. The women were also experts at foraging for the plants, fruits and seeds needed to sustain them through these long dark winter months.

If they had to follow the herds north there would be no guarantee that those plants they were familiar with would be available. Nobody knew what the earth so recently released from its icy prison would yield or if the new rivers would yet be stocked with fish.

The future was uncertain and Brynyar fell into a fitful and painful sleep as the fire in the hearth died down for the last time in his life.

The small clan led by the eldest son of Brynyar's hearth, packed up their belongings as soon as spring warmed the air in the valley. There were twenty five men, women and children all carrying heavy fur wrapped loads on their backs. With the women in the centre, the men and boys formed a protective perimeter, and as the days warmed they made slow but steady progress. Food was scarce in the beginning, but once they caught up with the herds they replenished their stocks and set up their summer camp near a river. They were delighted to find that there were indeed fish in the fast flowing icy water from the north and that the glacier melt had also nourished the surrounding land with its rich silt.

Scouting parties travelled north following the river to find a suitable winter cave and after two months they came across another clan on the same mission. They combined forces and discovered a series of large caves above the river valley about fifty miles from the summer camp.

With their wind dried meat, rendered fat, constant supply of fresh fish, foraged plants and seeds the two clans settled into their new homes. Over the years more strong and healthy boys with the clan marking were born. As the community grew, from time to time small groups from a hearth would move on. These bands bearing the mark of the clan travelled to all parts of the emerging continent; including across stormy seas to Britain and Ireland.

Present Day.

Brian Monaghan looked down at the sleeping child in his arms: his first great grandchild and the first Brian in the family for thirty years. He lifted the delicate right hand of the baby and smiled as he saw the familiar arrow birthmark. He and his sons all had this distinctive characteristic. The tales of why they carried this reminder of their ancestry had been passed down through the countless generations by mother to daughter and father to son.

No longer hunters, the clan had dispersed to the four winds and set up homes in villages and cities. However Brian's ancestors had remained nomadic, travelling through Europe entertaining all that they met with their acrobatic and athletic prowess. The group of families always returned here however to their winter camp in the southwest of Ireland to gather their strength, enjoy family life and prepare for the summer season of performances on the continent.

Brian held his great grandson in both of his hands above his head and twirled slowly on the sawdust covered ring.

'Today we welcome the latest Brian Monaghan to the clan and this fine strong and sturdy lad will one day take his place amongst you high above the ground.'

The baby's parents looked on proudly as their son chortled and waved his hands around as if reaching for the trapeze bars in the roof of the tent.

Another generation of the famous Monaghan Circus had made his debut.

CELIA

Celia sat on the edge of the wooden chair and looked around the sparse room. The bare white walls were cold and seemed to be closing in on her as if in reprimand for her decision. This room was not the only chilly environment that she had been subjected to for the last months, as news of her defection was whispered amongst those at a senior level.

She had been told to wait here over an hour ago. Her uncertainty about the future was now solidified into an icy premonition that she had made a huge mistake. This had been her life's work, her mission and her passion. At one time she would have walked across burning coals so strong was her belief, that the life she had chosen was perfect for her. For almost all of the last twenty years she had been an exemplary example of devotion to her vocation.

She had been named after her grandmother's much loved older sister. Great aunt Celia had entered this very order at fourteen years old and had died sixty years later as the Mother Superior of the convent. The younger members of the family had never been privileged to meet her. However, her grandmother spent many hours with Celia, talking about how proud the family had been of the devoutness of this legendary figure. Even as a child Celia had felt the weight of obligation and the need to honour the previous owner of her name.

Once in her teens and slightly at odds with the changing world around her; it became apparent to the devout Celia that she was destined to follow in the footsteps of her great aunt.

What's in a Name?

At age eighteen she had entered the convent and had never stepped outside of its high stone walls since that day.

Through the years as a novitiate and then following her final vows, she had embraced the life completely. The order rose each day at 5.00 am and spent the day in prayer and working within the convent and its gardens. When Celia retired each night to her small and austere room, she would remember her family in her prayers, even as their faces began to fade.

She couldn't identify the moment with any certainty, when doubts about her life resulted in sleepless nights, and loss of concentration during prayers. She found herself experiencing flashbacks to a time when her days seemed filled with laughter and light. Though frivolous, she also remembered teenage years and dancing with her sister to the latest hit record, as a brightly coloured skirt whirled around her knees.

She had tried to put these forbidden thoughts aside but she no longer felt peaceful or joyous as she dressed in her habit each morning in the cold dark of winter. She certainly no longer had the lightness of heart of the early years here in the convent. Like cracks in the dry earth these doubts had grown and spread through her being; until she could no longer be silent.

What she did feel was a huge sense of guilt. The thought of the shame that she was bringing on the name of her great aunt, who obviously had been far more steadfast in her devotion, consumed her. Her spiritual family here in the order would also be confused and hurt by her betrayal. She could only imagine how much her parents would be disappointed, and she dreaded the thought of facing them.

Across the room on a narrow iron bed, stacked in a neat pile, were the garments that she had worn daily for the last twenty years. As she looked at the folded robes and undergarments, she reflected on how little there was to show for all her time in the convent. She felt very strange in her new clothes that had been sourced from a store cupboard in the depths of the old building. Just for a moment she missed the all-encompassing safety of her former attire. She raised a hand to her short hair that felt coarse to her touch. It had been so long since it had been uncovered in public and its blunt cut and greying red hairs make her feel even more self-conscious.

The door opened and the Mother Superior stood in the doorway. She stepped back and beckoned Celia towards her, and watched as she bent to pick up the old brown suitcase by her side that held another set of equally dated clothes.

'Come along now,' she ordered crisply. 'Everyone is in chapel and you need to leave immediately.'

Celia brushed past the nun's voluminous black habit and the firmly clasped hands across her ample middle. There was no softness to be found there or comfort. Celia faltered for a moment and saw a slight shift in the older woman's stern features.

Closing her eyes she steadied herself against the door jam and then put one foot in front of the other. She clasped the handle of the suitcase tightly; in need of its rough texture against her palm to strengthen her resolve. In her other hand she gripped the white envelope which contained her official papers and a few notes to pay for her travel.

In silence the two women proceeded down the dark corridor and into the hall of the convent. One of the other senior sisters stood by the large oak front door and, seeing them approach, opened it to the front garden. Celia paused for a moment on the doorstep and turned for one last look behind her. Her biggest regret was not being able to tell her fellow sisters about her decision, or to say goodbye. She loved them all dearly and tears filled her eyes as she contemplated the future without their warmth and support.

The two nuns stiff postures softened for a moment; as they remembered times when their own faith had perhaps wavered momentarily. However, the rules were clear and gently the Mother Superior placed her hand on the small of Celia's back, and pushed her clear of the door. She then stepped back into the hall and there was a resounding click as the way back was firmly barred.

The sun was shining and for a moment Celia turned her face to the blue sky and warmth. She had been Sister Monica Grace for so long that even thinking about her given name confused her. Hands trembling as the fear continued its grip; she tried to move a foot down onto the first of the concrete steps leading to the garden. It was a long walk to the gate that separated the world from this enclosed order and she saw another sister waiting patiently to unlock and open it for her departure.

Gingerly she took her first step and then another and she managed to navigate the path to the walls behind which lay the outside world. Silently the nun used the long metal key and pulled back half of the tall wooden gate. Celia was too ashamed to look her in the eyes and slipped through the opening and onto the busy pavement.

Shockingly she was suddenly in a world that was noisy and filled with vehicles that looked alien. Pedestrians hurried along the narrow pathway and seemed oblivious to her standing in the middle of them. Especially those who were talking to themselves with some form of device held up to their ears.

Then she noticed a car parked at the kerb and a man waving his hand to urge her forward. She saw that the vehicle had the word taxi in big letters on the side and shakily moved

What's in a Name?

towards this life saver in the chaos. The driver took her suitcase from her and opened the back door. He smiled reassuringly and informed her that his cab had been booked to take her to the train station. Closing the back door firmly he took his place behind the wheel. As the car pulled away from the side of the road Celia took one last look at the high stone walls of her home for so many years.

∽∾

The driver navigated through the heavy traffic whilst his passenger gazed around her in bewildered confusion: so many cars and people, and a blur of colour as shops and restaurants flashed by the windows.

Within minutes however they arrived at the station and she was shocked to see Margaret waiting for her on the kerb. How was this possible? She had not taken advantage of the offer to make a phone call to her family, in her certainty that they would not be accepting of her decision. The driver came around to her side of the taxi and held the door open with the battered suitcase in his hand. As her sister rushed forward, Celia grasped the top of the window and pulled herself out onto the pavement. Without any hesitation her sister leant forward and throwing strong arms around her shaking body, held Celia tightly.

The two women stood back after a few moments, and holding hands, looked at each other in wonderment. Celia reached out a palm and laid it on her sister's soft cheek. It was like looking at a mirror image; but one that was brighter and lighter than her own. Soft curly red hair with just a few strands of grey shone in the sunlight and the green eyes with traces of tears sparkled back at her.

'How did you know where I would be?' she stroked her sister's arm.

'Mother Superior called me a week ago and told me that you were not going to call us,' Margaret paused. 'How could you think that we would not want you to come home, Cel.'

Celia subconsciously moved her fingers through her hair and Margaret laughed and hugged her close.

'First stop the hairdresser when we get home.' She stood back and looked at Celia's old fashioned tweed suit. 'And we need to get you a new wardrobe.'

She gently released her sister's fingers from her hand and picked up the suitcase lying abandoned at their feet.

'I have missed you so much Cel. Only once a year for twenty years is torture.' With that she placed her arm around her waist and they moved off into the station.

∽

The train flashed through the countryside at terrifying speed but as the two sisters sat side by side the ice cold fear in Celia's chest began to thaw.

She let her twin rattle on brightly about her house, her husband Robbie, the two boys Andrew and Patrick who Celia had never met. Margaret had also brought a large envelope of photographs of all the family, including her parents, surrounded by grandchildren and pets in their back garden. Celia touched her sister gently on the arm to pause the exuberant flow of words.

'Do they understand Mags?' she bit her lower lip.

'They love you Cel and have your old room ready and waiting,' Margaret leant over to kiss Celia's cheek. 'They have missed you so much and whilst they respected your decision to enter into the convent, they never really forgave grandmother for encouraging you.'

Celia didn't take her eyes off the face so like hers as she continued to relate the events of the last twenty years, embellishing the stories in a way that she had almost forgotten. She felt bathed in the warmth of the outpouring as she watched her sister's lips moving, entranced by the unfamiliar sound of a voice talking rather than praying.

For the last few miles of the journey they sat in silence basking in the sunshine that shone through the carriage window. They held hands as they had so many times as children; a closeness that only twins share. Celia had sat in silence when at prayer thousands of times in the last twenty years, but she finally realised that the missing element had always been this closeness. The simple joy of being with each other, knowing that there is love and an unbreakable bond between you.

She had no regrets about her life and her chosen path but she also now understood, that when joy has left and cannot be recaptured, you needed to let go and move forward in a new direction.

She also pondered the unexpected kindness shown by Mother Superior in notifying her family. She had been so terrified of taking this step that she had forgotten the compassion that her religious sisters offered to each other as part of any close knit family.

The train entered the station and the two sisters walked arm in arm along the platform until they were swallowed up and smothered by kiss and tear filled embraces from the welcoming committee.

CLIVE

The boy stirred in his cot and waved his chubby fist in the air. The mid-afternoon sun was barred from his room by the rattan blinds at the window. The slowly moving blades of the fan above his cot sent a welcome and cooling breeze across his hot skin. The rest of the house was quiet, except for the gentle snoring of his amah as she dozed fitfully on the pallet on the other side of the room.

The boy was called Clive and was the fourth child and first son of a naval officer and his wife who were stationed here in Trincomalee. He was three years old and his curly blonde hair now lay slick against his scalp as he recovered from the fever. It had been a worrying few days with the doctor calling in every few hours to check on his condition. The household, including his three older sisters and his parents, were exhausted having had little sleep for the last few nights.

Measles in this climate could be very dangerous for a child Clive's age and he had been restricted to his cot in the darkened room to prevent the risk of blindness. Thankfully his fever had now broken, and the family having enjoyed their Sunday curry lunch, had retired to their bedrooms to sleep the afternoon away beneath their ceiling fans.

Clive had been woken every hour or so to sip his favourite fruit juice and water from his beaker and the doctor was now happy he was past his crisis. But, the child was now hungry and the lingering smell of the chicken curry that the family had consumed at lunchtime drifted into the room.

What's in a Name?

Relieved that her charge was out of danger but extremely tired, his devoted amah had failed to latch the side of Clive's cot securely. Seeing that there was a means of escape; he lifted his body up into a sitting position and swung his bare legs over the side of the mattress. It was easy enough to slide down onto the stone floor with its fibre matting where he held onto the side of the cot for a few minutes; his legs wobbling beneath him. But he was a strong little boy who spent hours on his tricycle and swam most days and this was evident in his recovery from this recent illness. Of course his growing hunger was a great motivator.

Carefully he moved across the matting intent on seeing if his friend the family cook had a special plate of his favourite mild curry and banana. He moved into the hall but was disappointed that the door to the kitchen was firmly closed and the handle was out of reach of his eager fingers.

The door to the long veranda however was much easier to open and Clive pushed his way through into the stifling heat and the raucous sound of the monkeys in the trees in the garden. He loved the little macaques and often sat on the veranda in the cooler mornings and watched them play fight over the ripened fruit. He drifted across the wooden floor and down the two steps onto the dusty path. He was now in uncharted territory.

There were many dangers for humans in these luscious surroundings. Clive was accompanied everywhere by his amah or his sisters when out of sight of his protective mother. Several times he had been scooped up and rushed indoors accompanied by shrieks and calls for the houseboy to bring a stick.

Cobras were common; as were the larger less playful monkeys that could be as big as dog. The first lesson that Clive had received after he had taken his first steps, was not to touch anything with fur, as rabies ravaged both the wild creatures and domesticated dogs.

With the fearlessness of a three year old, he toddled down the dry dusty path until he reached a line of ants that were busy carrying leaves several times the size of their bodies across the dry earth. Fascinated Clive sat down on the ground and followed their progress with one little plump finger.

Eyes were watching him from various vantage points in the overgrown garden. The small macaques ceased their play fights and spotted that the door to the house had been left ajar. This was as good as an invitation and a dozen of the petty thieves scampered down their favourite tree and darted along the edge of the dry lawn and through the bushes beneath the veranda. In seconds they were through the open door looking for food and mischief.

In the branches of a tall evergreen, a large male langur watched his smaller cousins disappear and waited to see if they would emerge with anything worth stealing from them. He had more sense than to risk the wrath of a house boy armed with a broom. Then something else caught his eye in the bushes to the side of the lawn. He stared for several moments trying to find the cause of his disquiet. His attention was then drawn to the chortling of the child as he played in the dry dust with the ants.

Something was wrong and the langur's instincts caused him to move cautiously to the end of the branch that stretched out over the lawn. There was the movement again and this time he saw the hooded head standing tall surrounded by the red blossoms of the rose bush. Slowly the cobra slithered from its hiding place and moved gracefully across the bleached grass towards the oblivious child.

Clive became bored with watching the ants and his hunger reminded him that the cook might be in the kitchen.

What's in a Name?

If so, then his favourite sweet treats, that were slipped to him occasionally behind his mother's back, might be on offer. Placing his hands firmly in front of him he pushed his bottom into the air and then stood unsteadily for a moment. A movement in the corner of his eye made him turn his head and he found himself just feet away from the swaying hood of the cobra. Without someone to sweep him up into safe arms and rush him inside the house he was minutes away from certain death.

In those precious seconds as the boy and snake stared at each other there was a sudden and violent interruption. The large langur launched himself from the branch of the tree landing a few feet from them. Without a moment's hesitation the monkey raced across and grabbed the tail end of the cobra. With one sweep of his powerful arm he swung the snake around towards the bushes several feet away and let it go.

For one moment the child and the monkey looked into each other's eyes and Clive raised his hand as if he understood that his saviour meant him no harm.

At that moment shrieks and angry shouts erupted from the open door to the house and the troop of macaques raced out with their trophies of chapatti and trifle filling their hands. Behind them, with an agility that belied his age, was the irate cook wielding a large kitchen knife. Under cover of the confusion the langur headed rapidly to his tree to resume his watch. The cook seeing Clive still standing on the path called out for his amah to come quickly and within moments the child was safe in loving arms and being hugged and kissed.

Soon the whole family congregated on the veranda and reviewed the damages to house and the theft of the left overs with a welcome pot of tea. None the wiser about their youngest child's close encounter with nature, they watched as Clive ate a bowl of home-made ice-cream.

Present Day.
The tall silver haired man drove up and parked at the back of the large manufacturing plant. He got out and opened the back of the van and approached the double steel doors and rang the bell to the side of them. A disjointed voice requested his name and after a moment the buzzer indicated that the door was open.

Inside in the dim cool the man walked up to a reception desk and was taken through to a holding area where six large wooden crates were waiting. Having lifted the lids of the boxes and checked contents, the man signed numerous pieces of paper. Two burly porters helped carry the crates out to the van where they were carefully placed and secured for the journey.

Four hours later the van arrived at a location deep in the countryside and having called ahead, several people stood clustered around the large open gates. Clive sighed with relief and drove through and backed the van close into a large wooden building.

The contents of the van were unloaded and the crates carefully carried inside. The markings were clear in the dim light from the outside lights at the entrance.

Contrux Pharmaceuticals.

Clive and his team gently lifted the sleeping occupants of the crates out and placed them in individual stalls lined with straw and soft bedding. They would be carefully watched by them in turns for the next few days around the clock. They would be fed and given water as well as checked out by the resident vet. It would take weeks, if not months, to rehabilitate these primates who had been born within a laboratory environment. However, with love and care; one day they would be enjoying their new and natural habitat.

What's in a Name?

As Clive laid the final animal in its bed of straw the chimpanzee stirred and for a moment he and the man looked into each other's eyes. A flash of understanding passed between them and slowly the monkey's eyelids closed as he was laid gently onto a welcoming blanket. A child and his destiny had now come full circle and his debt would continue to be repaid as long as he lived.

DIANA

Diana Grace was an only child of two older parents who had been delightfully surprised when they discovered that after fifteen years of marriage; a baby was on the way. Her father was a professor of music and her mother a psychiatrist and Diana had grown up in a household filled with love and laughter.

Not wanting their daughter to be the stereotypical only child, her parents had made sure that she understood that achievements and money only came through hard work. Diana had started with a paper round and moved on to work in the local bakery as a counter assistant through school and then university. Despite her parents being well off, they insisted that she contribute a part of her weekly take home pay towards her upkeep and it was with great pride that she handed over those few pounds per week.

Being a bright and outgoing child opened doors for Diana and after completing her degree in English Literature; she was offered the job as assistant manager of a large bookshop in Oxford. This meant a move away from her parents into a shared house with three other young women all beginning their careers away from home.

The next two years passed quickly with Diana enjoying her job and also a hectic social life with the group of close friends that grew around her. She managed to get home to see her parents at least one weekend a month and they watched as she blossomed into a vibrant and beautiful young woman.

What's in a Name?

One day Diana looked up from the counter where she was checking in a batch of new books to find herself staring up into the face of a very good-looking man. Tall, with dark hair that fell naturally across a broad forehead down to full and smiling lips, to a dimple and a very masculine chin.

She realised that she had been staring and gathered herself quickly.

'Good morning, how may I help you?' Diana placed her hands on the counter in front of her in what she hoped was a professional manner.

'Hi, I'm looking for a copy of Great Expectations for my nephew's birthday; do you have a recent edition in stock?' As if aware of her discomfort the man tilted his head to one side and looked her directly in the eye.

There followed a romance that would be termed whirlwind, with Diana swept along in the passion and certainty that she had only read about in books. Within six weeks she had taken him home to meet her parents and three months later they were married in the church a short walk from her parents' house. She became Mrs Simon Forester and she repeated her new name several times a day in an effort to remind herself of her good fortune.

Simon was a merchant banker and worked in London. He already had a flat in the Docklands and after the wedding Diana moved in with her many boxes of books, music and the wedding gifts. Ecstatically happy, despite leaving her close friends behind, she went job hunting and found a book shop in Holborn who was in need of a manager.

The whirlwind did not stop as the social life that Simon's work provided was fast and addictive. She adored her handsome husband and secretly enjoyed the looks that other women would cast in their direction when they walked into a room. The only slight niggle that Diana had, was that her

What's in a Name?

parents never seemed to warm to Simon. When they visited for a weekend or special occasion there was a tension that worried her.

It was just after their third anniversary that a crack appeared in their marriage. Diana had thought that their celebration dinner was the most appropriate time to tell Simon that they were having a baby and that she was two months pregnant.

He had placed his glass of red wine down on the white tablecloth very carefully and turned his cold gaze towards her excited and radiant face.

'How did you let that happen?' he spat at her as she sat open-mouthed at his reaction.

Flinging his napkin down on the table he called the waiter over and demanded the bill. Taking her arm far too firmly in his clenched hand, he virtually frog marched Diana from the restaurant and out to their parked car.

A frosty silence descended on their marriage with Simon working long hours and declining to discuss the baby in any form. Eventually in desperation Diana cornered him after he had returned in the early hours of the morning, clearly drunk, and asked him what he wanted her to do.

After a moment's silence he turned to her and for a moment she saw a flash of a smile but not one of charm.

Diana lay in the bed and the pain radiated up from her leg through her body to join with the pounding headache. She could hear sobbing and her hand lying limply by her side was being gripped tightly. As her eyelids fluttered open she felt warm breath travel up her arm across her neck and then close to her ear.

'If you say one word, I will make sure that I finish the job next time,' she shuddered with the menace dripping from his voice.

'You became dizzy and fell down the stairwell outside the flat, do you understand me you stupid piece of garbage.'

Terrified Diana tried to pull her arm out of his grip and then heard another voice from the end of the bed.

'Time to let your wife rest Mr Forester and you look as though you need to head off and get some sleep yourself.' The brisk tones of the nurse indicated that this was not a request and Simon stood up and patted Diana's arm.

'Alright darling, I'll see you in the morning,' he turned to the nurse and flashed his most charming of smiles. 'Look after them for me please sister; they mean the world to me.' With that he brushed past the nurse and left the ward.

Despite the pain, Diana's first thought was for her baby and weakly she reached out to the nurse. 'Please is my baby okay, I have to know, is it safe.'

The nurse moved down the bed and laid a gentle hand on Diana's shoulder.

'You have a lot of bruises and a concussion but luckily you fell onto your side. Your stomach is bruised, but the baby is fine and strong, so try not to worry.' As she continued to carry out various checks, the nurse looked down at Diana's bruised face.

'You know that if you need help, in any way, there are people we can call,' she paused. 'That was a very nasty fall that you had and it would not be good for you or the baby if that happened again.'

She placed the lead with the call button into Diana's hand and satisfied that she had done all she could for the time being she walked down the ward to talk to the doctor.

The pain medication was beginning to take effect and although drowsy, Diana knew that this was a time for clear thought and action. It was not just herself that needed protection but her unborn child. She had never experienced true anger before in her life but she now realised that this pressure in her chest and her head was not just a result of Simon pushing her down the steps outside their flat.

It was a deep seated and instinctive need to protect the life of her unborn child.

The next morning, having been called in the night by the ward sister, Diana's parents sat by her bedside holding her hands and talking quietly to each other. The door at the end of the ward was flung open and Simon strode down the marble floor bearing a bunch of red roses and smiling at the nurses in passing. He looked ahead and saw Diana's father and mother and the smile froze in place.

As he came closer, he noticed another man slightly hidden by the curtains who walked to the end of Diana's bed. Simon glanced at his wife as she lay propped up against her pillow and was met with coldness and determination that he found surprising.

He heard footsteps approaching firmly from behind him and the roses fell to the floor as his arms were wrenched behind his back.

Struggling against his captors he turned to face the stern-faced man in front of him.

'Simon Forester, I am arresting you…

DAVID

David stood beside his comrades as they waited in the village square for the parade to begin. Despite their advancing years, the men stood as tall as possible, often with the aid of a stick. Two of their number were in wheelchairs, and had been guided across the cobble stones by their fellow old soldiers.

It was a typical chilly November morning with dark skies and clouds laden with imminent rain. Whilst inappropriate perhaps for this solemn occasion, the men standing huddled against the cold wind; wished for a few rays of sunshine. Their overcoats were shiny with age but their shoes were burnished to brilliance thanks to the loving attention the night before. A reminder of a time when the action of rubbing in polish, and then shining the boots for the sergeant's approval, was used for reflection. A time to remember all the nights, many years ago, when comrades would sit on camp beds talking quietly as they prepared their kit for inspection and parades.

Beribboned pins, holding silver and bronze medals, lay proudly against the material on their chests and nobody really noticed the frayed cuffs that peeked out from the sleeves of the worn coats. Their pride was clear to see by all who passed; many of whom smiled in recognition or tipped a hat. They were the old soldiers and heroes of the village and despite their dwindling numbers were respected and honoured. Not just today, but every time they were met in the shops and lanes of this small community that had given up so many of its young men to war.

David did not feel the cold and felt content to be part of the camaraderie and fellowship of being amongst those he had served with. He caught little snippets of conversation as he stood, head bowed waiting for the order to form into the parade.

'My Elsie has had another grandson… Who would have thought it…? I'm a great granddad….'

'That new doctor looks like he's just left school… Told me that I had something called heemaroids… Used to call them bloody piles in my day…'

'I'm sorry that Jack didn't make it this year… Miss the old codger… We will have to find a replacement for the cribbage night…'

David smiled as he listened to his friends talking about their lives and raised his head as he heard the sound of the local brass band strike up.

He had been part of this ceremony for the last fifty years since the squire had erected the memorial in the centre of the village. Lord Roberts was a good man and had been devastated by the loss of his own son in the last few weeks of the war. Out of respect and loyalty to those other families in the village and surrounding area who had lost fathers, husbands and sons, he had paid for the monument himself.

That first November as the group of survivors had stood in the rain to commemorate the loss of their brothers and friends, many had still relied on crutches, and as today, one or two had been in wheelchairs. It was a far cry from the day that they had stood in this same square waiting for the horse drawn carriages to take them off to basic training.

The call had come, and from the surrounding farms and isolated cottages, men between the ages of eighteen and thirty-eight, who were not exempt because of occupation, health or marital status, walked proudly into the recruitment centre in the village hall. David was just nineteen when war was declared and was swept along by the patriotic message and fervour that swept the nation. There was talk down the pub of places outside of their small community that might be visited.

'Blimey, a chance to see the other side of the hill lads...' and 'Do you think those French girls are as friendly as they say?'

The thought of glory and adventure had been foremost in their young minds. It certainly did not hurt that the girls in the village became very attentive when they arrived back for leave after basic training in their uniforms. The day that they had formed up into a parade, to march to the square and climb aboard the transports, was frozen in time. Mothers weeping as they clung to their sons and fathers slapping them on the back and proudly straightening their caps. Couples embracing for one last kiss and whispered words of love.

It had been very different when David returned to the village a year later. Although now only twenty he felt that he had aged a lifetime. As he stepped down from the train in the nearby town, carefully favouring his injured right arm and struggling with his kitbag, it was without glory. The sight of his parents waiting from him in the evening sunlight had reduced him to tears and as the horse and cart made its way to the farm; his mother had held him tightly as he sobbed against her best coat.

Over those first few days of calm and peace; David had spent hours alone walking the fields and hills desperately trying to find any meaning behind the senseless carnage and sacrifice he had experienced. He knew that once his injury was fully healed he would have to return and the thought of this kept him awake at night in his room in the rafters of the farmhouse.

What's in a Name?

Then one day, as the sun shone as he helped his father harvest the wheat, he saw his mother heading towards them swinging a laden lunch basket. Beside her with golden hair that gleamed in the sunlight was a tall and very beautiful young woman.

'Here you go pet,' his mother handed off the basket to David. 'You remember Cathy from the Black's farm don't you?'

David looked into bright blue eyes and was then drawn down to the perfectly formed red lips that smiled at him.

Six weeks later they were married in the village church and had walked out into the sunshine to a guard of honour of fellow soldiers home on leave, or who had been injured. The reception in the hall in the square had been packed with well-wishers and David and Cathy had danced and celebrated until midnight. Then they had slipped away unnoticed to their room above the pub.

Every year since the memorial was erected David had marched with his comrades and then stood with them as wreaths were laid around the base. And each year his breath would catch in his chest and his heart would skip a beat as he watched his Cathy carry a wreath and lay it amongst the rest. That first year she had also held the hand of a little girl, his daughter who unlike all others sombrely dressed, was wearing a beautiful handmade coat of blue. His favourite colour.

He had watched Cathy and his daughter every year since then as they would both walk proudly to the memorial and lay their tribute. But this year his daughter walked with another by her side and there was no sign of his darling wife. He slipped through the ranks of his comrades until he was standing in the front row. He could hear his daughter saying something to the tall young man by her side.

'You lay the wreath David; your grandmother wanted you to do it for her this year.'

What's in a Name?

The lad reverently laid it down amongst the others and he stood back by his mother's side. Together they turned and walked solemnly back towards the waiting villagers where they were greeted with hugs and the boy was patted on the back.

A tear rolled down David's face with sorrow at the loss of his beautiful Cathy. As he stood bereft at the front of his silent comrades at attention, but with their heads bowed, the clouds parted and rays of sunshine spread across the square. As they did so, his eyes were drawn to a young woman with golden hair and blue eyes who walked over the cobbles to stand by his side. She slipped her cool hand into his and he smiled down at her with joy.

Unseen by all those who had gathered to remember him and all the others who had not returned; they slipped away hand in hand. The long wait for them both was over.

ELAINE

Elaine lay under the warmth of the duvet and her hand crept across the mattress to touch her husband's hand. Not enough to wake him but just a gentle touch to remind him of her presence. Jack's even breathing and gentle snore was comforting and Elaine smiled to herself, savouring the delicious secret that she was desperate to reveal.

She had been saving up the news until today as a gift for Jack's birthday. They had been married for two years and she knew that his greatest wish was for them to have a baby. His large family had already provided his parents with six grandchildren and whilst he might not talk about his desire for a family; he wanted to hold their child in his arms almost as much as she did. She had remembered the look on his face when she had thought that she might be pregnant but it had turned out to be a false alarm.

This is why she had waited until she was absolutely sure; today would be the perfect time to reveal the secret.

Jack stirred beside her she turned her face in anticipation of his usual morning kiss on her brow and lips.

'Good morning my lovely,' he gently stroked some stray hairs out of her eyes. 'How are you today?

Elaine smiled at him lovingly and touched the tip of his beautiful nose. 'Happy birthday my darling,' and she leant over to kiss his mouth.

Over breakfast they discussed the final details of the birthday party that afternoon. Jack's family lived too far away to attend but he had asked one of their neighbours from down the street to join them. Jessica was always in and out and would pop in for coffee most mornings when Jack was at work. Sometimes she would also bring her children in at the weekend and they had a wonderful time playing scrabble and cards.

Elaine had butterflies in her stomach as the urge to blurt out her special secret became too much to bear. It had to be the right moment, when Jack was cutting his birthday cake that Jessica had kindly made for him. She was a much better baker that she was and it looked amazing.

Jack had been in the navy when they met and on top of the white and blue cake, a figure in a sailor's uniform posed with an anchor. Elaine bet the inside of the cake would be delicious and would taste all the better when she announced her news.

After a quick sandwich for lunch and whilst Jack tidied the living room ready for the party, Elaine popped upstairs quietly to their bedroom and sat at the dressing table. She smiled to herself as she viewed her reflection in the mirror. There was no doubt about it; her skin had a definite glow. Artfully she brushed her blonde hair into a smooth bob and applied her makeup carefully. Not too much, but just enough to enhance her youthful beauty. Laid out on the bed were three outfits and Elaine was having problems deciding which to wear. Jack would always laugh about her preparations for an evening out. He knew she would try on all the options a couple of times before making her final choice.

This kept her busy for the next half hour and eventually she headed downstairs in her favourite cream dress with pearls at her neck and in the lobes of her ears. Jack took her hands and stepped back for a better look.

'You look stunningly beautiful sweetheart,' he gently straightened the string of pearls around her neck; they had been his wedding present to her.

What's in a Name?

Elaine almost gave the secret away at that point but held the temptation in check. Her plan was perfect and she must wait a few more hours until his birthday cake was cut.

Jack left her sat in the lounge surrounded by plates of neatly cut sandwiches and a pile of festive napkins. In the corner on a cabinet sat the cake surrounded by the birthday cards that had arrived over the last two or three days.

Just then the doorbell rang and it startled Elaine as the sound intruded into her secret daydreams. She pushed herself out of the chair and headed for the hall. Jack was coming down the stairs and held out his hand to her.

'Don't worry love I'll get it,' and he opened the door to find their three guests on the doorstep.

In they came, bearing brightly coloured bags of gifts and contributions to the birthday tea. There was much hugging and chatter as overcoats were dispensed with and they all headed into the living room. Jack and Jessica took the food she had brought into the kitchen and put the kettle on. Sophie and Ben, who were in their early teens, entertained Elaine with tales of their antics at school during the week.

The food disappeared rapidly and two pots of tea later it was time to cut the cake. This was Elaine's moment and she stood up to join Jack at the cabinet as he prepared to slice into the blue and white icing.

'Darling, I have a very special birthday present for you,' she held out the envelope that clearly contained rather bulky contents. Jack smiled at her eager face and proceeded to open the envelope carefully. He drew out the birthday card that had a huge heart on the front and carefully opened it to reveal the surprise. In his hand was a pair of knitted baby booties decorated with white satin ribbon.

Tears formed in the corners of his eyes as he pulled Elaine to him. 'Thank you darling for the best birthday present I have ever received.' Over her shoulder he smiled at their guests and they nodded and smiled in return.

Jessica's children helped clear away the plates and carried them into the kitchen whilst their mother sat on the sofa holding Elaine's hand. 'That is wonderful news and I am so happy for the both of you.' She smiled gently at the woman at her side. 'We can talk about it on Monday when I pop in for coffee and we'll get the baby knitting patterns out to look at.'

An hour later and Jessica kissed Elaine on the forehead and gently stroked her cheek. She headed off to the hall and gathered up the coats and handed them out to Sophie and Ben. When she reached the front door, she turned once more and gave Jack a warm hug and whispered in his ear. 'It was a wonderful birthday tea Dad and I will come in as usual on Monday when you go out to do the shopping.'

Jack went back into the lounge and stood for a moment looking at his wife, sitting calmly watching the flames flickering in the fireplace. The outfit that Elaine had finally chosen was her wedding dress, and she looked as radiant today as she had forty years ago. He sat beside her and gently moved some stray silver hairs from her forehead and took her face in his hands. He looked into her sparkling blue eyes that no longer recognised her daughter or grandchildren.

The most precious birthday present he had received today, was that his beautiful Elaine still knew him, and that even in the darkness, her light continued to shine brightly.

ERIC

Eric stood in front of the mirror and for a moment deliberately avoided putting his glasses on. All he could see was a blur and therefore could just about pass muster. Behind him he could feel the presence of his wife Billie and knew what she was going to say.

'Eric, love you have let yourself go,' there would be disappointment in her voice.

He slipped his spectacles on and his image immediately appeared all too clearly. He did a quick head to toe scrutiny. Muddy red hair streaked with grey, too long about the ears and hanging over the neck of his dressing gown. Three days' worth of beard as he only shaved once a week when going to the supermarket for the shopping. His tatty t-shirt that he wore over his ancient pyjama bottoms sported faded lettering that read Grateful Dead; his slippers had a hole where his big toe poked through.

Yes, Billie would have definitely gone to town on him.

He debated whether to pull the bedroom curtains or not and decided to leave them for two very good reasons. Firstly, letting daylight in would illuminate the state of the room which was a shambles and secondly, it might signal to Mrs Green across the road that he was alive and would welcome her advances.

He left the drapes undisturbed and shuffled out onto the landing and down the stairs to the chilly hall. Damn, he had left the kitchen window open again. He wasn't bothered by burglars since there was little of value to be taken except for his photograph album, and that was safely locked away behind the big seascape on the dining room wall. The safe also held a few precious mementos, such as the leather box that contained Billie's few bits of good jewellery; her bling as she called it. Her engagement and wedding rings, some earrings she had inherited from her mother and a watch that he had splashed out on for their 25th wedding anniversary.

He wandered into the kitchen and put the kettle on and measured out some oats into a bowl with some water. He stuck that in the microwave and closed the offending window that had let the cold night air into the house. Three pings announced that his porridge was ready and he threw a tea bag into a mug of boiling water. There was a few inches of milk in the bottle in the fridge and he poured some over the oats and into the mug. That left enough for a coffee later, but having forgotten to put the item on his list three days ago; it looked like he would have to venture forth after all to the shop on the corner.

He carefully carried the bowl and mug into the dining room and stopped dead. There, sat on one of the dining-room chairs was a cat. A ginger and black cat to be exact and it was looking at him expectantly. Eric nearly dropped the bowl and tea on the floor and just managed to reach the table, laying them down before he slopped hot liquid all over his hands.

His visitor remained impassive and kept eye contact, which rather disconcerted Eric who was not used to animals, especially cats. Billie had been allergic to them and since they had travelled a great deal, particularly when he had retired from the police force, there had never been an opportunity to bring one into their home.

The cat was virtually the first visitor to the house in the year since his wife had died. One or two of the neighbours had popped in with shepherd's pie or offers to come to Sunday lunch, but after several polite rejections had given up on him. Except, of course, for Widow Twanky across the road who was looking for husband number four. Perhaps his having been a copper had a bearing on the lack of neighbourly communication. There was no doubt that they liked having one on the street as a deterrent to some of the criminal fraternity, but socialising was quite another thing. You never know what guilty secret might slip out after a couple of glasses of wine.

His friends from the force had tried to encourage him out of his self-imposed exile too, with telephone calls asking him to join them at their old watering hole, The Bugle. He just couldn't face their sympathy or the awkward silences in the middle of a busy night in the pub. Eric was also terrified that he would embarrass himself by blubbering into his beer at the first kind word.

Since the cat was making no move to vacate the chair he usually sat on; he moved to the other side of the table and placed his now cooling porridge in front of him. The creature was still giving him the once over and then offered its opinion in the form of an elongated meow that sounded rather unflattering. Eric raised his hand to his shaggy head and tried to smooth his hair into place. He felt very disconcerted by the direct gaze of his uninvited guest and thought perhaps an offer of some of his porridge might divert its attention.

There was a saucer on the table under a dead house plant that looked reasonably clean and he carefully poured a little of the lukewarm porridge with its milky topping onto the china. He laid it down in front of the cat and watched to see if this would be acceptable. With impeccable manners it delicately placed two front paws on the table and gently lapped at the offering; still keeping both eyes firmly on its host. Eric shrugged and proceeded to eat his breakfast and drink his tea, also keeping eye contact with his feline intruder.

Several days passed and Eric got into the habit of leaving the kitchen window open each night. Every morning he would poke his head around the door to the dining room and sure enough his new companion would be waiting on the chair expectantly.

In the first two or three days the cat would leave its designated chair and disappear into the kitchen after consuming its own bowl of porridge. Eric could hear the faint sound of paws on the marble surface; followed by the sound of a slight scramble as it left through the open window. He was surprised to feel a sense of loss.

It was not long before the visitor, who Eric had named Doris, was dropping off the chair and crossing to the sofa where she would settle herself in to sleep away the morning. She might pop out of the window from time to time but always returned to the warm patch she had fashioned for herself. Eric had established by careful scrutiny, that Doris was indeed a girl and that he had not insulted some tetchy tomcat; within a few days she would lift her head when he called her name.

Eric found himself shaving every morning as he needed to go out more often to buy fresh milk and also tins of cat food. He began to open the curtains in his bedroom and the washing machine began to hum in the background more often. Doris would sit in a patch of sunlight in any of the rooms that he happened to be in and gradually over the next month both man and house came back to life. A visit to the barbers and a rifle through the sale items in the supermarket had resulted in some new clothes, slippers and also a couple of pairs of pyjamas.

They lived together but remained aloof. It was to be six weeks before Doris approached him as he sat leafing through his photograph album on the other end of the sofa where

What's in a Name?

she normally lay. He tentatively put out his hand and stroked the top of her head and then down her sleek back which she obligingly arched. She nudged closer and he placed his arm around her. He was amazed by the loudness of the delighted purr that vibrated in her chest. He looked back down at the album open to the photographs of his and Billie's wedding day forty five years ago. It was the sixties and his long red hair hung down to his shoulders; his lovely Billie who had only been twenty at the time had sparkled in her cream dress and fake fur cape. She used to call him her Viking warrior, and would tell him as they lay in each other's arms at night how safe he made her feel.

Tears filled his eyes and they dropped onto the plastic film that protected the photos. Some splashed onto the hand that was holding his warm companion close to him and he felt her rough tongue lick the moisture away. He smiled down at her and then gently wiped the tears from the album. Billie's last words to him had been to beg him to find happiness again one day and not to live alone. He took his arm from around Doris; closed the album firmly and placed it on the table beside the sofa.

'How do you fancy a bit of tuna for supper Doris?' He rubbed a tender spot beneath her chin. 'Then I have to pop out for a couple of hours to meet some old work mates down the pub.'

FIONNUALA

Fionnuala Garvin was pinned to the wall of the toilet block. Her small body was pressed back onto the cold red brick as her shoulders where firmly clamped beneath the stubby fingers on grubby hurtful hands. The pain from this mauling was excruciating, as her white blonde hair was trapped beneath the vicious fingers and her scalp felt like it was on fire. With her fragile swan-like neck, slight frame and skinny legs she did not look twelve years old and right now she wished she was back in primary school where life had been so much kinder.

Her lower lip trembled and she tried not to cry as the onslaught continued unseen by the teacher on monitor duty in the playground. This was Ciaran Walsh's favourite spot for tormenting the younger children and extorting their lunch from them, and today he was in an even worse mood than usual. Not the sharpest knife in the cutlery drawer, at fifteen he was failing a number of subjects. Just this morning he had been sentenced to a week of detention for failing to hand in an essay for his history class. He was looking to take out his rage on someone.

Fionnuala or Nola as she was known to her friends was terrified. Normally there would have been two rounds of cheese sandwiches and an apple in the satchel now lying at her feet, but today she had forgotten to pick the brown paper bag up from the counter in the kitchen at home. Without these essential bargaining chips, she was going to be in for a hiding.

Ciaran's breath smelled rank. His stained teeth offered plenty of evidence of what he had eaten for breakfast and lack of an acquaintance with a toothbrush. He brought his cavernous mouth close to Nola's terrified face and spat out his demands.

'Fionnuala Garvin. You are mine and I own you. Give me your lunch now or I will pinch your arms until they are black and blue'. He sneered viciously and pressed further into her body.

Just then large hands descended on Nola's attacker's upper arms and he was virtually lifted into the air and shoved back out into the playground. Ciaran steadied himself and poised for a counter attack but stopped abruptly in his tracks. He looked up into the eyes of a tall and well-built senior from sixth year and knew that he would be hard pressed to better him in a straight fight. The older boy stood protectively in front of Nola and, with a quick check to make sure his young charge was not hurt in any way, he turned back to Ciaran who was still mulling over his options.

'Ciaran Walsh I know how to find you and it won't be just me next time, you need to get your sorry act together. Get back to class and I will be watching your every move from now on; just feck off.'

The disgruntled bully turned and nonchalantly headed off back into school and tried to ignore the smirks on the faces of the bystanders who had witnessed the altercation.

Unfortunately as he reached the steps leading up to the main entrance, he tripped and almost fell; gales of laughter followed him as he hurried through the wide blue doors.

Meanwhile Nola's rescuer put a consoling arm around her shoulders and steered her towards her classmates. They had remained huddled together awaiting the outcome of this daily assault on any of their members foolish enough to get separated from the pack.

What's in a Name?

'Listen to me,' the tall lad addressed the white-faced group. 'My name is Patrick Flanagan and you must come and tell me if this happens again. He smiled at his new devotees. 'My friends and I will do our best to keep that one out of trouble in the future.'

He left unaware of the admiring glances and excited whispers behind him.

Ten years later Nola checked herself in the mirror before heading downstairs; she never grew tired of seeing herself in her Garda uniform. Following her training she had been posted to this town in the heart of a farming community and after a year in the job she could honestly say that there was little she did not enjoy. She went downstairs following the aroma of scrambled eggs on toast with a rasher of bacon that her husband Patrick had laid on the table. He turned from the cooker with his own plate and they sat across from each other eating leisurely and enjoying this rare breakfast together. He was a doctor at a hospital in the nearby city and their shift patterns did not always allow for regular meals; when they did manage to get time it was precious.

He kissed her goodbye and watched her through the kitchen window as she backed her car out of the drive. He had some time before his shift started and as he cleared the breakfast crockery away he reflected on what a lucky man he was. Who could have thought that the little blonde waif that he had rescued that day in the playground, would end up becoming his wife. He was very proud of her and knew that she had passed every examination and physical test with flying colours. That did not however stop him from worrying about her safety, especially as he saw the results of violence associated with crime on a far too regular basis.

The object of his thoughts was not unaware of her husband's concerns and that drove Nola to even more excellence when it came to training and attention to detail. She had two hours before her shift began and she was headed to a physical training session with her partner on the force. He might be a great friend to both she and Patrick, but once they hit that mat they would fight hard for the win.

Dressed in her sweat pants and t-shirt, Nola faced off against her partner. They circled each other waiting for the slightest move that would indicate an attack. Although taller and broader than Nola, her opponent was light on his feet and his muscled body moved agilely across the mat.

Seeing what he perceived as an opening; he reached out and managed to place a hand on Nola's shoulder. The next thing he knew he was on his back with one arm held upright; his hand bent forward in a tight grip.

Nola leant forward close to the face of her partner who was grinning up at her with his killer smile; the one that had the girls falling at his own feet.

'Ciaran Walsh, you are mine and I own you. Buy me lunch or I will pinch your arms until they are black and blue.'

FRANCIS

Francis Baxter checked into the hotel in the middle of Chamonix on the Friday night, and tired from his long journey, headed off to bed and slept for ten hours straight.

He woke to find the sun streaming in through the windows of his suite and a craving for several cups of strong coffee. He showered and sat in the extremely fluffy bath robe supplied by the exclusive hotel and waited for room service to send up his breakfast. He closed his eyes and took a deep breath. He didn't want to think about Chrissie back home in Houston or Dane and Shannon finishing off their semester before heading home for the Easter holidays. He hadn't informed anyone, not even his business partner of twenty years, where he was going; he had not switched on his mobile since landing in Geneva yesterday.

Unfortunately denial did not stop the rush of thoughts and emotions that had been triggered two days ago when Chrissie had asked for a divorce. Their discussion, that had developed into a full-blown argument, replayed in his head over and over. Her accusation that he was more interested in his work and making money than their marriage, and that she no longer loved him had established itself front and centre in his mind; he had not seen that coming. He knew that he was ambitious and he and Richard, his partner, worked long hours keeping their accountancy business afloat in these uncertain times. Yes, they played golf at the weekends but it was their way of unwinding after a long week. He admitted

What's in a Name?

to himself that there were too many dinners in the city with major clients but they required constant attention. The fact was that without the business they would not have the big house, fancy cars and vacations. He had thought that Chrissie was content with the trappings that came with his job; he was furious with himself for missing all the signs and taking so much for granted.

There was a discreet knock on the door and Francis walked over to admit the uniformed waiter who wheeled in a laden trolley. Having slipped the young guy a generous tip, Francis settled down at the table and contemplated his breakfast. Suddenly he had little appetite so sipped his strong black coffee and flicked through one of the local guides that were spread out in front of him.

The truth was that he knew this area quite well as he had lived here as a child with his French mother and American father who was an artist. They had moved to the United States when he was twelve years old, which is why, when faced with this bombshell he had chosen to run as far as he could; to somewhere he still considered his home. A picture captured his attention as he automatically turned the pages in the glossy brochure. It was of a place that he remembered from his childhood when he and his parents would take long treks at the weekend up the sides of the surrounding mountains. His father would carry the rucksack containing their lunch which always consisted of a fresh baked baguette from the local cafe along with fresh tomatoes and a tub of rich homemade mayonnaise. They would find a perch above the valley and the three of them would break the bread into chunks, add a dollop of mayo, a couple of slices of the bright red tomato and it tasted heavenly.

This reminded him that he was actually hungry right now. He decided to tuck into the now cooling omelette and croissant; he was going to need some fuel for the walk he now planned to take.

Francis opened his suit carrier which he had hurriedly thrown random clothes into and realised that he was not equipped for hiking. He pulled on some jeans and a sweat shirt and headed downstairs and out into the main street. The shops didn't open until later in the morning, but he spent his time well, window shopping and popping into a bakery for another coffee and some supplies for his hike. He returned to one of the sports outfitters that he had scoped out earlier and bought some jeans, boots, parka and a rucksack. He also picked up a detailed guide to the trails, not trusting his memory completely, and a water bottle. He returned to the hotel and quickly changed into his new clothes. At the last minute he added his mobile phone to the essentials in his rucksack for safety reasons and headed down the corridor to the elevator.

Two hours later after realising how out of shape he was, Francis breathlessly reached his destination. The roar of the torrent of water that rushed down the mountainside from the spring melt filled the air and the scent of pine was strong in his nostrils.

Memories flooded back of a different time when every spare moment that he had was filled with activities like this. His parents always seemed to be there beside him hiking, skiing and sledding down moonlit slopes close to the town. He remembered drinking hot chocolate around the fire at a local inn and being included, even when there were adult guests around the big kitchen table for fondue. What he could not remember was the last time that he, Chrissie and the kids had spent any time together or even enjoyed a family meal.

He viewed the narrow footbridge across the gorge that he needed to cross to reach the small building clinging to the

What's in a Name?

rock face on the other side of the raging river. It had carried thousands across safely over the hundreds of years that it had existed but a little hesitantly he walked over, watching the flood waters racing beneath him.

Francis thought he knew what to expect as he opened the door into the little chapel, but was still unprepared for the wave of emotion that swept through him. Sunlight fought to gain entry into the tiny space through small windows fashioned into the thick outer wall. The faint rays illuminated the walls of stone and the shrine at its heart. Francis walked slowly inside and stood for a moment with his head bowed.

Around him in the cracks in the walls, hundreds of small slips of paper caught the light. They were the prayers and supplications of people across time that had needed guidance and restoration of faith. Townspeople had walked up from the valley and travellers through the passes had stopped for a brief respite and comfort. Their combined presence had created a vortex of emotion and the hair on the back of Francis's neck stood on end.

He had never been a religious man but he knew that this place was a spiritual oasis where all could regain their strength and sense of purpose. He remained for a few minutes longer and then gently closing the door behind him he walked back across the bridge.

Gradually the feelings that had been triggered so forcefully subsided and in their place came clarity.

He walked down the trail until he reached a point overlooking the town. He sat on a warm rock and opened his rucksack. He broke the baguette into four pieces and liberally spread fresh mayonnaise on each piece before adding a thick slice of tomato with a little salt. He ate his simple meal as he contemplated his next move.

What's in a Name?

Satisfied now in body and soul he picked up his mobile and switched it back on. Ignoring all the texts and messages waiting for him; he made two calls. The first to Chrissie that lasted a long time and ended with his satisfied smile; the second that was equally lengthy to his business partner. He packed up the remains of his lunch and headed back down into the town where he spent the next few hours visiting chalet rental offices

For the first time in years, Francis felt that he was where he belonged and a huge weight was lifted from his shoulders. Chrissie would be arriving tomorrow and then next week Dane and Shannon would join them. It was time to repair those bonds that had been broken and to forge new ones that were stronger and would last a lifetime.

GRACE

It was Grace's fifth birthday and the staff at the council run orphanage had made sure that there was an iced cake for tea and some small wrapped presents beside the plastic yellow plate. The children sat at tables for ten boys and ten girls and meal times were expected to be conducted in silence. This rule was however broken on birthdays, when all fifty children would stand up and sing Happy Birthday enthusiastically in the hopes of receiving a thin slice of the oblong sponge cake.

Grace sat in silence as the noise erupted around her and gently fingered the blue and white wrapping paper on the nearest present to her. From the shape she could see that it was a book. It would not be new; a hand me down from one of the older children. Still, in this home of abandoned children, a gift was always treasured. A tear rolled down her flushed cheeks and slid into the corners of her mouth. She wiped them away hurriedly; being a cry baby was frowned upon. Gratefulness for the charity that put a roof over your head and food on the table in front of you was drummed into the children from a very early age.

The energetic rendering of the song ended and there was a scrapping of wooden chair legs as all fifty children sat down at once. Silence resumed as slices of bread and butter were grabbed and placed onto plates with well-scrubbed hands. There were four small dishes of jam around each table and the youngest children would wait their turn knowing that receiving a small spoonful would be an unusual bonus. One

What's in a Name?

of the serving ladies, a local girl called Alice, took away the oblong iced sponge cake to be cut into thin slices. After the Grace had been served one of the pieces; the large platter moved around the dining hall watched eagerly by fifty pairs of eyes.

Picking at the cake with trembling fingers, Grace managed to eat a few morsels before a coughing fit overtook her. The matron came across and slapped the child firmly on her back and offered her the beaker of diluted orange juice.

'Come on girl, buck up,' the stout grey-haired woman looked down at her sternly.

'There is many a child here who would be delighted to have these treats'

Grace tried her best to smile knowing that being labelled ungrateful brought consequences and having been disciplined twice recently, she was in no hurry to repeat the experience. It was not seen as cruelty to stand a child in a corner for an hour at a time or to send them to bed without even this meagre supper. Grace had felt the pangs of hunger more than once since her best friend Hope had left the orphanage.

The thought of her friend waving goodbye as she had left in her smart new tartan coat, made Grace catch her breath. To stop herself crying she pinched her arm as hard as possible. She hoped that Hope had not forgotten her now that she had a real mummy and daddy. The two girls had been brought to the orphanage within days of each other at only six weeks old in the winter of 1953; as toddlers they had become inseparable.

They were so very different that no-one could mistake them for sisters. Grace had straight red hair that frizzed at the slightest dampness and freckles sprinkled her nose and cheeks. She grew rapidly into a gangly five year old whilst Hope, with her curly blonde hair and blue eyes, remained petite and doll-like. It was always hoped that the babies who

What's in a Name?

arrived at the orphanage would be adopted into a good home. Although there had been some interest initially, by the time the two girls reached four years old it was becoming more and more unlikely that this would happen.

However, a few months ago a couple had arrived and immediately taken to Hope and started the proceedings to adopt her. The two small girls had known nothing but this regimented environment, and never imagined that one day they might be separated so devastatingly.

The matron rang the large brass bell on her table. The children stood ready to file out to the games room for an hour before bedtime at seven o'clock. Grace trailed behind the other girls from her table clasping her three gifts; as yet unopened. As the older boys played with some wooden toys in the corner, some of the smaller children clustered around Grace and begged her to open the presents. As expected there was a dog-eared picture book of fairy stories which was passed around and admired. One of the other packages contained a small packet of sherbet sweets that were eagerly sampled and in the third was a woollen scarf in a bright red colour. Grateful for its warmth, Grace wrapped around her neck and sat until bedtime looking at the pictures in her new book.

Grace had barely eaten since her birthday and the head teacher at the primary school in the village had rung matron to say that the child was becoming more and more withdrawn. Although strict and somewhat fierce looking, the matron was not an intentionally unkind woman and she called in the doctor from the local surgery.

He was a gruff looking man with a shaggy mane of greying hair. The children adored him because he always arrived with pockets filled with boiled sweets. He sat on the edge of Grace's bed and having examined her carefully, he took her little hand in his.

What's in a Name?

'Well little Grace what a pickle we are in,' he smiled down at the solemn child. 'It is nearly Christmas and you will miss all the fun if you don't start eating soon and you will have to stay in bed.'

The child turned her head away and whispered into her pillow. 'I only want Hope to come back home for Christmas.'

The doctor returned downstairs and met with matron behind the closed door of her office. Reluctantly at his request she made a phone call and proceeded to have a lengthy discussion with the person on the end of the line.

Having left instructions that Grace was to be fed every two to three hours with some chicken broth and a little toast and jelly if she would eat it, Doctor Baxter left to continue his rounds. He promised to return on Christmas Eve in three days to see how the patient was doing and also to carry out his annual duties as Father Christmas at the children's party.

Grace did sip a little of the broth and nibbled at the toast and three days later she was carried downstairs and sat on a chair near to the Christmas tree. The children had made all the decorations and what they might have lacked in expertise they had made up for with bright colours and glitter. Fairy lights flickered through the branches of the tree that had been donated by the villagers along with a present for every child in a sack placed by a big red arm chair. The presents were to be distributed before they would sit down to unusually overflowing platefuls of sandwiches, jelly and as a very special treat, Christmas cake. The boys and girls were not sure what they were looking forward to most.

Hearing tyres on the gravel of the drive the children rushed to the windows of the dining hall and started clutching each other in excitement. Santa Claus sat in the back of a large open topped black car and when the vehicle stopped; he opened the door and stepped out to wave to them all. They were so focused on his progress as he walked to the front door that the three other passengers in the vehicle went unnoticed.

Ten minutes later Santa was sat in his large comfortable chair and the children came up one by one to sit on his knee and were given a present wrapped in festive paper, tied with either a blue or pink ribbon. Grace watched the proceedings quietly on the side lines until there was just one present left. Alice put down the jug of juice that she was serving to the children and came over, picking Grace up and depositing her gently on Santa's lap. The white faced child glanced up into a pair of twinkling eyes that looked vaguely familiar, but it was difficult to tell who was behind the big white bushy beard.

He leant down and whispered in her ear. 'I hear that you would like something very special for Christmas, is that right little girl?' He winked at her. 'I hope that I've brought you what you wished for.'

At that moment Grace's eyes were drawn to three people who had suddenly appeared at Santa's shoulder. For a moment she froze in place, then pushing herself off his knee, she wrapped her arms around the small blonde girl standing in front of a smiling man and woman.

The two girls remained huddled in each other's arms sobbing uncontrollably until the woman knelt down beside them and wiped their faces with a clean white handkerchief. Satisfied that she had managed to stop the flood of tears, she reached out and took each of their hands in her own.

'Hope has missed you dreadfully Grace and we have heard so much about you,' she smiled at the bewildered Grace. 'We were all hoping that you would like to come and live with us too; as Hope's sister.'

An hour later the group of adults watched as the two girls sat side by side at a table. They were talking non-stop except when selecting and eating another sandwich or a piece of cake.

What's in a Name?

Even matron could not hold back a smile at the change in Grace now that she was reunited with her soul mate. As for Santa, he scratched his face behind the itchy beard and wished that he could capture this moment for ever.

GEORGE

George Horsefield slowly pushed open the door of the garden shed and poked his head through the narrow opening. He slowly scanned the immediate vicinity to make sure that the dog that lived in the house behind him was not lying in wait. It was a motley small mongrel with sharp teeth and there had been a couple of occasions when those teeth had connected with his legs in a very unpleasant manner.

All seemed safe and George eased himself out onto the garden path that led to the wooden gate, but not before a quick glance behind him for a last look at his beloved.

He and Mildred had been having a torrid affair throughout the summer months with secret assignations in her shed or his own. However recent events made them both aware, that for the time being, their trysts would have to come to an end.

Both structures had been cleared out and then cleaned and prepared for the coming cold months. Lawn mowers had been taken apart and oiled after the final grass cutting of the year and had been stored in one of the corners. The floors had been swept and mousetraps laid to protect the bags of seed stored on the top shelves. Old grain sacks had been pinned across the window to prevent the intrusion of any winter sunshine and the doors would be locked to prevent gale force winds from blowing them open; curtailing their delightful activities.

Mildred was sleeping peacefully, partially covered by the old plaid blanket that had kept them warm and protected their

What's in a Name?

modesty should anyone enter the shed unexpectedly. George smiled to himself contentedly and could not help adding a little swagger to his walk down the path. No bad for an old codger he thought to himself as he poked his head out and checked the pavement for anyone who might know him.

The coast was clear but he knew that any minute now the mothers would be arriving to pick up their children from the primary school on the corner and the area would become very busy. Hugging the hedge he moved carefully, lifting one uncooperative leg after another; muttering under his breath at the stiffness in his slightly bent knees. His earlier smugness at his athletic prowess began to fade as he struggled to cover the distance between Mildred's house and his home. He had two garden lengths to go when disaster struck.

Ahead of him he saw the aforementioned dog sniffing her way along the pavement, lost in the scents that assailed her delicate nostrils. George knew from his previous encounters that the monster would recognise his smell within the next few minutes; coming after him without mercy. He looked to the right and noticed that his next door neighbour's gate was slightly ajar; with a gentle nudge he slipped rather ungracefully through the gap. He didn't want to risk the dog following him so he pushed the barrier shut with his backside. Hearing a welcome click, he manoeuvred carefully behind the shelter of the hedge, waiting breathlessly for the animal to pass.

Outside on the pavement the dog had definitely got wind of her foe. She knew that George was up to no good in the shed and it was her job to protect the house, garden and family; including Mildred. She sniffed the air and her eyes were drawn to the closed gate. Barking madly the frenzied demon pushed and snarled at the obstacle.

All it did was draw the attention of her master who was walking along behind her carrying the afternoon paper. She felt

What's in a Name?

her collar being grasped firmly and was then frog-marched along the pavement and into her own garden. All she could do was whine in disappointment as she stuck her nose through the bars of the closed iron gate.

Meanwhile George was weak-kneed with relief and had to take a few minutes to recover. The pavement was beginning to fill up with mums on their way to pick up their children and rather than risk being seen, he decided to take a short cut through a large gap in the hedge that he had discovered recently. As he began to ease through the foliage he realised that it was only just in time; it was clear his absence had been noticed. He might have been a bit of a Jack the lad with Mildred but he felt he had just cause. The mother of his children, boys he loved dearly, was a fire-breathing dragon of the worst kind and through the evergreen barrier he could hear her shouting.

'George, come out wherever you are,' she paused for a moment obviously scanning his usual hiding places. 'Come along you dirty old devil, I have got better things to do than chase you about the place.'

The subject of her ire stayed stock still; poised in the middle of the hedge waiting until he heard the slam of the kitchen door. It was now safe to make his laborious way across the uneven lawn. Carefully he tip-toed into the gloomy garden shed and feigning sleep, he settled down waiting to be discovered.

A few minutes later he heard childish laughter and running feet heading for the house. He knew that after a tea of beans on toast and rice-pudding with strawberry jam he would be joined here in the shed by the three lads. Sticky fingers would nudge him awake and he would be given delightful cuddles and regaled with the adventures of the day.

What's in a Name?

He was dozing happily, dreaming of Mildred and their next encounter, when he felt himself lifted up into the air and gently deposited into a large plastic box. Beneath him he could smell fresh garden compost and he wiggled his toes as he settled himself down. A lid was placed over the container and through the holes above him he could hear the one of the children whispering to him.

'Goodnight George, sleep tight and see you in the spring.'

Then the dragon spoke. 'Thank goodness for that, at least we will know where the old boy is for the next few months. I swear I never knew that a tortoise could be so much trouble.'

HANNAH

I sat in a corner of the pub nursing my sparkling water and lime juice. The Sunday lunch crowd was growing by the minute in this popular country inn; already there was loud laughter and raised voices of the customers competing with the background music.

We had first frequented the pub to sample their renowned Sunday lunch buffet over thirteen years ago, shortly after our marriage and move to the area. Two years later when our son Michael was born, he had been seated in one of the oak high-chairs supplied by the pub for their younger patrons. I smiled as I remembered the look on his face when handed his first roast parsnip. Distrust swiftly followed by a smile of delight as the crispy outside gave way to the soft sweetness. He was never a picky eater and I loved watching him discover new foods and tastes once he moved onto solids.

It was an 'all you can eat' buffet which was highly dangerous, especially for my husband Tom, who could rarely resist the temptation. As he sat contemplating his empty plate; I would run through the desserts up on the blackboard in an effort to move him on from the roast potatoes, but rarely succeeded. He always had room for apple and blackberry crumble; especially with piping hot custard poured liberally over the top of it. Michael was into ice-cream and usually opted for a scoop of all three flavours available. In the early days the evidence of his dessert was clearly seen around his mouth and down the front of his shirt.

What's in a Name?

As his sixth birthday approached I brought up the subject of a party for his friends and was firmly put in my place. 'Mum,' he looked firmly into my eyes. 'I want to go to the pub with you and dad for my birthday like every Sunday.'

I rang ahead and reserved our usual table and having mentioned that it was Michael's birthday, the manager offered to have a birthday cake made. When we arrived there had been helium balloons attached to the backs of the chairs and a banner on the wall behind the table. I have never seen such delight on my son's face as the assembled Sunday crowd sang him Happy Birthday. Most of them had seen him grown into this fine young boy and it was just the perfect day.

The noise from the bar interrupted my train of thought. The pub had changed hands about four years ago in my absence. I had been surprised when I had walked through the door to see no food being served and a completely different atmosphere. There were few families; just a four deep crush around the bar area and loud music playing discordantly in speakers at each corner of the room. Something had not changed however and I recognised one tall man who stood head and shoulders over those he was drinking with. He looked like the life and soul of the party and it was clear that his enraptured audience of middle-aged men were very happy for him to keep putting his hand in his pocket and paying for another round. Raucous laughter created a moat around this particular group as other patrons, excluded from this select few, moved further away towards the tables along the walls.

The man had been here on the day of Michael's birthday party and had been the only discordant note of the day. Loud and brash he had dominated the crowd at the bar as he was doing today, knocking back several neat whiskies in the space of an hour. In fact it was his behaviour that had encouraged us to leave earlier than usual having indulged in birthday cake topped with Cornish dairy ice-cream. The staff kindly packaged up the remaining half of the cake, and with one very happy birthday boy clutching the box in his hands, we headed home.

I remember that drive as if it was yesterday. My son strapped into his booster seat behind us still clasping the remains of his cake; my husband humming along to one of the CDs playing some jazz and turning occasionally to smile at me. The weather was not great with freezing rain beginning to coat the dry roads. Tom was a careful driver and slowed down as we navigated the narrow country lanes between the pub and our village five miles ahead.

Suddenly there was a blast of a car horn behind us and Tom looked into the rear view mirror at the vehicle that had suddenly and rapidly appeared around the curve in the road. Tom rarely swore and certainly not in front of Michael so his 'What the bloody hell....' both shocked and scared me. I looked over my shoulder to see a long sleek Jaguar sports car almost on our bumper; Tom slightly eased ahead as he approached the next bend. We had nowhere to pull into as a wall of granite stretched up on one side and there was zero visibility ahead. That however did not deter the driver behind us as he accelerated passed us across the solid white line and into the curve.

Tom and I saw the oncoming car at the same time and I screamed as it swerved to avoid the Jaguar and slammed straight into us at speed.

I was in a coma for five days, watched over by my sister Janice who had arrived from her home in Paris. Despite my injuries, I insisted on attending the funeral of my husband and beautiful son. I did not cry.

I did not cry at the inquest; or the subsequent trial of the man who had caused the accident. I had been able to give the police enough information about the distinctive car for them to track it down to a house at the other side of our village. This was not the driver's first offence but armed with an expensive and clever lawyer he claimed mitigating circumstances: including putting the blame on Tom's slow and careless driving. In the end, despite his blood alcohol level and his dangerous driving, he only received a seven year sentence and a driving ban of ten years.

I had moved away from our home as I couldn't live with the memories we had created together. I moved to the city and went back to work as a chemist in a large pharmaceutical company. I lived in a sterile flat with just the photographs of my husband and son and rarely sought out the company of others outside of work. I knew that Tom would be disappointed in me and that he would only wish that I would go on with my life and find love again. But there was no space for another love until I had received justice for those I had lost.

I came back to the present as the tall man at the bar threw back the contents of the glass of whisky and slammed it back down on the counter. He slapped a few of the men on the back and sauntered to the main door. I left my half-filled glass of water and lime juice and followed him out into the car park. I knew which car was his as I also knew which direction he would be taking. Although I had moved from the village my neighbours had kept me in touch with his movements; including the party he had thrown himself when he had been released two years early for good behaviour. It was clear that he had not taken his punishment seriously or the fact that he was still banned from driving for another five years.

I had counted every whisky that he had drunk this lunchtime and as he fumbled for his keys beside his car I approached him from behind.

'Excuse me,' I smiled as he turned to face me. He showed no sign of recognition despite seeing me in court every day of his trial. My long dark wig and sunglasses were more than adequate a disguise considering how drunk he was.

'How can I help you sweetheart,' he leered at me suggestively.

'I know there's a police speed trap around the first bend out of the village,' I lied through clenched teeth. 'I thought you might like a spray some of this breath freshener just in case they pull you over.'

'Thanks babe,' he held out his hand for the small aerosol. He opened his mouth wide and winked at me as he squirted a healthy dose onto his tongue. He handed the spray back to me and I headed to the car that I had borrowed from a friend. I sat behind the wheel and watched as he too slipped into the driving seat. After a few minutes I started my own engine; as I slid passed the Jaguar I smiled with satisfaction. He was slumped back in the seat clutching his chest and gasping for breath. I carried on driving out of the car-park and onto the road that would take me back to the city.

Two days later the paper carried the story about a local man convicted of dangerous and drunk driving that had killed a father and six year old son; found dead from a heart attack behind the wheel of his car outside a popular public house.

Three months later I sold my flat and moved to the West Country where I bought a coffee shop with the proceeds called Hannah's. On Sundays I served an 'all you can eat' buffet with a wide selection of Cornish ice-creams. At last I could move on with my life.

HECTOR

Hector Gonzalez looked out of the plane window, over the wing and across the bright blue sky. Just in sight, dark clouds gathered beneath them and the captain had activated the seat-belt sign with a warning of possible turbulence. With two hours left of the flight from Mexico City to Las Vegas, and the airline magazine read from cover to cover, there was more than enough time to contemplate what was waiting for him on arrival.

The last time Hector had been to Las Vegas was thirty years ago as a college kid. He lived in San Francisco with his parents who had emigrated from Mexico when he was a baby. His dad had worked on one of the fishing boats that headed out into the bay each day, captained by his Uncle Pedro, who had lived in America for twenty years.

His mom had worked in his Aunt Maria's restaurant and he certainly had warm memories of the fajitas and quesadillas that made their way home at the weekends. It was a great childhood and his parents never let him forget how fortunate they were to be living in this city, so different from their lives in Mexico where his grandparents still lived.

In the early days it was tough to keep in touch with the family that remained in Chihuahua, but letters and parcels were exchanged and when his grandparents had a telephone installed it was like Christmas to his mom and dad.

Hector turned to look at the man sat next to him but could see that he was not interested in a conversation. He was staring at his laptop screen; writing what looked like a report of some kind. The seat-belt sign was switched off which triggered the resumption of the refreshment service. Within minutes the attendants had reached his row and asked Hector if he cared for anything. He smiled, refusing politely and turned his head away to stare out across the never-ending sky.

Almost thirty years ago to the day over this holiday weekend, Hector and his friend Cesar had decided to use the break from community college to drive over to Las Vegas, picking up Cesar's cousin Jorge in San Jose on the way. His mom and dad were not happy with the choice of destination. Las Vegas was a town that might appear cosmopolitan at that time, but whilst there were many Hispanics in the service industries, there were not so many at the gaming tables. However, the two boys promised that they would stay in a decent motel off The Strip and would avoid getting into trouble.

They threw their bags into the back of the car and headed out on a glorious spring morning to pick up Jorge and complete the nine hour trip in time for dinner. They arrived in Las Vegas and drove around the outskirts until they saw a reasonably smart looking motel with both vacancies and cheap rates for family rooms. They booked for four nights and were very happy with the large, clean room with three beds and set about getting ready for a night on the town. Jorge was twenty-one and the other two were big strapping lads; buying beer was not a problem in the bars off the main drag.

After a few drinks they made a quick stop at the burger joint down the road then, with their saved cash burning a hole in their pockets, the three boys headed into one of the smaller casinos to hit the slot machines.

Two hours later they decided to move on having won a hundred bucks between them. Enough to cover their motel bill and some left over for food. Delighted they wandered down the main drag enjoying the bustle and lights that brought the place to life after dark. There was some debate about hitting more slots but both Hector and Cesar were tired from the early start and drive and they voted to return to the motel, starting fresh again in the morning.

They had just turned around to retrace their steps when they saw a commotion up ahead of them at the entrance to one of the bigger hotels. A man was waving his arms around and pushing a number of security guards who were attempting to eject him onto the street; the boys moved closer to watch the action. Force of numbers eventually ended the tussle as the uniformed men propelled the offending customer out of the big glass doors and towards the spectators who had gathered. There was a certain amount of laughter as the man tripped and fell to his knees but this turned to gasps of shock as he stood and pulled a gun from his pocket. Hector and his two friends froze in place on the side-lines as shots rang out on the now silent street; two of the security guards fell to the ground.

The crowd scattered and as sirens could be heard approaching from the north of the casino, the shooter turned and ran towards the south and right into the crowd including the three boys. For a moment he was face to face with Cesar as the boy stood in his path unintentionally blocking his escape route. He brought the gun up and stuck it into the terrified boy's chest and smiled slightly as he began to pull the trigger. Instinctively Hector charged from Cesar's right; punching the man hard in the side of his chest. He stumbled and before he could recover, Hector grabbed his gun arm and they struggled for possession of the weapon.

Hector was oblivious to everything around him. The screams from the crowd, the sirens, even the sound of his own breathing until the noise of the gunshot shattered the silence in his head. He expected to feel pain, but there was none. He expected to fall but he was held in the embrace of the killer who was staring into his eyes. But, suddenly the man's gaze wavered and he slipped slowly to the ground to lie lifeless at Hector's feet.

A day later Hector waited in an interview room for his parents to arrive. A detective sat across from him and asked him if he understood everything that he had said. Hector nodded silently. The door slammed back into the wall and his mom rushed into the room, around the table grabbing him tightly in her arms. His father stood helplessly by the doorway, white-faced and unmoving.

Within a week Hector was living with his grandfather in Chihuahua and working in his Uncle Julio's garage. The house was basic but it was safe and it would be unlikely that the mob would find him here amongst his extended family and their community.

His name had not been released but it was always possible that someone would be bribed to provide the name of the killer of the eldest son of one of the most powerful mob bosses in Chicago. Even the police in Las Vegas had not wanted to know where he was going. They were satisfied that it was self-defence and a murderer had been taken off the streets. He was slipped across the border into Mexico having said his tearful goodbyes to his parents and two friends.

It was hard to believe that it was thirty years ago and how much his life had changed. But not as he had thought as he had entered his grandfather's house for the first time. At that moment all he could think about was what he had given up; having no idea how much he would gain. The family of aunts and uncles welcomed him with open arms and outside of work he found himself caught up in a whirl of fiestas and family celebrations where he met his lovely Maria. They

What's in a Name?

had been married for over twenty five years and had three fine sons who all worked with him in his flourishing garage business in Chihuahua.

His parents had come back to Mexico when his father retired and lived close by in one of the new gated communities. Although so many dreamt of a better life in America; they relished in coming home to the warmth of their extended family and grandchildren.

Today Hector was going to a reunion. He had kept in touch with Cesar and Jorge over the years and this weekend they were going to be staying at one of the brand new resort hotels and casinos. It would be tough for him to revisit this place where his life had changed so dramatically. It had been several years before he had stopped looking over his shoulder and even now he occasionally felt he was being followed. However the mob boss was long gone and the world was a very different place. When he had received the email from Cesar he had almost refused but Maria had persuaded him to go, meet his old friends and put the past to rest once and for all.

The captain announced that the plane was coming into land and illuminated the seat-belt sign for their descent. After a smooth touchdown the plane taxied to its stand and the passengers filed out of the front door. After passing through passport control and collecting his suitcase, Hector made for the exit into the concourse and into the toilets to freshen up before finding a taxi to the hotel.

A man followed him through the doors into the almost empty restroom. Hector went to wash his hands and turned his head to the man at the next sink. He was surprised to find it was the passenger who had sat next to him on the plane; now wearing a baseball cap and long black coat. The man turned to him and smiled and the next moment Hector felt a sharp pain in his side; looking down he saw his companion's hand clenched against his chest. As his vision began to fade he saw the hand withdraw holding a long narrow blade. He clung to the sink as he felt the warm breath in his ear.

'That's for my brother Hector.'

ISOBEL

Isobel Smith looked out of the window of her thatched cottage at the small garden that fronted the narrow lane. She would have to rake up those leaves soon. They would start to blow around the house in the blustery wind that came off the sea most days.

The issue was finding the time between the autumnal downpours that plagued the coast at this time of year. She chuckled to herself as she contemplated this activity and wondered when she had become such a sissy. After all it was only rain and not likely to kill her.

It was Halloween, and when Isobel had been into the post office in the village the other day, the post mistress, Agnes Flanagan, had reminded her that the handful of children left in this small outpost on Finnegan's Hook, would be trick or treating tonight. Agnes had suggested that she buy a couple of packs of the fun size chocolate to fill the buckets that accompanied the costumed tricksters, and good-naturedly, Isobel had popped the bags into her shopping basket.

Her life here was vastly different from the one she had left behind. A high flyer, Isobel had definitely raised the glass ceiling as far as women in her profession were concerned. She had been in demand around the globe and had a reputation of being able to resolve complex and seemingly impossible issues decisively and cleanly. She could have lived anywhere in the world on the proceeds from her long career, but with an instinct honed in the cut and thrust of her chosen profession, Isobel knew that a quiet, out of the way retreat would be

What's in a Name?

the perfect spot to settle. She kept a low profile, avoiding the quiz night at the pub and did not venture onto social media, preferring instead to walk the coastal path every morning and watch re-runs of Midsomer Murders every afternoon.

She didn't lack for company however as she had recently adopted a three-legged black cat called Lucky. He had a squint which meant he never quite met her eye, but in her career she had found that was also the case with people she had come into contact with. As she contemplated the leaf raking task and the upcoming trick or treating, Lucky jumped up onto the back of the sofa at her side and sidled up for a stroke to his arched back.

Later that afternoon, Isobel gave some thought to another problem that Agnes had divulged when she was in the shop this week. Agnes was oblivious to the fact that she was renowned as the village gossip and cheerfully dispensed everyone's personal business to all who would listen. Isobel would normally filter out these minor snippets and nod knowingly from time to time, but something caught her attention.

'Well you know, there have been six cats gone missing in the last month and everyone is terrified about letting them out at night.'

Isobel had paused and looked up from examining a new line of cat food on display.

'Do they have any idea what is taking the pets?' Placing her hand firmly on the post office counter, Isobel looked pointedly at Agnes.

'Well…. I don't like to speak ill of people… but there is talk that it is Patrick Feeney up to his old tricks.'

With Lucky's safety to consider, Isobel was not going to let the matter drop there, and she eased the rest of the story from the obliging postmistress.

Apparently, Patrick Feeney was a vicious thug who had terrorised the children in the small village primary school before going to the secondary school in the nearest big town. He had been shipped off to a young offender's institute at age 15 after being caught breaking into the village pub one night. There had been talk at the same time of cats going missing and wildlife being found mutilated and left outside homes in the village. Those disturbing and hideous activities had stopped when Patrick was away serving his sentence for burglary, but had resumed again very shortly after his release.

Isobel's thoughts had returned frequently to the matter over the last few days. As she heard his rich and throaty purr, and felt Lucky's bravely beating heart, she decided that nothing was going to happen to her only true companion.

That night the children of the village dressed as spiders, skeletons and witches and knocked on the doors of the cottages that surrounded the square and lined the lane to the beach. They were accompanied by their parents, but when they knocked on her door, Isobel could sense that there was an element of watchfulness and fear to the adults' vigilance. She dispensed the various fun sized chocolate bars into the proffered buckets and the noisy group moved onto the next cottage down the lane; laughing excitedly and comparing their hauls.

Locking the front door behind her, Isobel headed off in the opposite direction to the revellers. She left Lucky looking out of the brightly lit window; no doubt surprised by his owner's rare excursion into the night. Swiftly and with purpose, Isobel walked across the square and headed down the lane that led to the farmland to the north of the village. The road also passed the house owned by the widow Feeney and her recently returned son Patrick. Despite the cold wind, Isobel tucked herself into a small break in the hedge

What's in a Name?

on the village side of the cottage, and with hands in pockets waited patiently.

The next morning the villagers woke to a bright and sunny day and discovered, as they went about their daily business, police cars and an incident van parked in the square. Knowing that the person to question was to be found behind the counter of the post office, a crowd gathered and shot questions at a delighted Agnes.

'Shush will you ever let me say my piece,' she admonished the agitated group.

'It would seem that Mr Kavanagh was walking his dog Betty along the beach this morning and found a body.' Pausing for effect, she pronounced authoritatively.

'I hear tell it is that rogue Patrick Feeney who must have fallen during the night when out on the prowl.'

Over the coming weeks there was a great deal of speculation about the demise of this detested and feared member of the community. Everyone commiserated with Patrick's mother, who to be fair, seemed to be relieved by the incident, and she began to thrive as she became the centre of attention in the village. She had been so mortified by her son's previous behaviour that she had imposed isolation on herself; even to the extent of shopping in the next village down the coast.

As Isobel was a relative newcomer she was not questioned by the police or her neighbours about the event. She therefore did not disclose her observations of the dead man on the night in question; which would have confirmed that he was indeed guilty of crimes against the domestic animals in the area. Nor did she feel it necessary to detail her actions following those observations.

However, one lucky tabby cat had been returned home to scurry through a cat flap and lick its sore ear with a likely determination never to leave its fireside again.

What's in a Name?

Over the next few years Isobel was taken into the heart of the village, and those who sought her expertise never discovered her sanctuary. But, in high places and low dives around the world, many wondered what had happened to the highest paid and most successful assassin of all time.

IFAN

Ifan Williams sat in the small velvet chair that usually held his gran's dressing gown and woollen shawl. The green velveteen gown was now draped over the end of the bed; adding some extra warmth to her feet as she lay sleeping deeply on this winter's afternoon.

The big double bed was one of the few pieces of furniture in the cottage overlooking the estuary, when David Lloyd had carried his young bride, Megan, over the threshold in 1920. Over the next few years, other pieces, usually made by local craftsmen, had been carefully brought in through the wide front door at the end of the stone path that led from the main road. None of those hand crafted pieces had been replaced in the last fifty years; the sturdy old oak bed was no exception.

His gran lay beneath a patchwork quilt that she had made as part of her bottom drawer. She had explained that expression to Ifan during their nightly chats by the fireside where they sat together after supper. His granddad had died when Ifan was just three years old; whilst he was living far away in South Wales with his mother and father and two older brothers. He had never known him, but Ifan knew his face well from the old photograph above the mantelpiece: a stern looking man with a big bushy moustache and eyebrows, who Ifan was just a little afraid of.

Gran had laughed at this notion and set about telling him tales of his granddad and his life on the mountain. Cadair Idris was on the other side of the estuary, where David had tended sheep for a large landowner all his

What's in a Name?

working life. She told Ifan of his laughter and the way he would pick her up and swing her around the small kitchen when he came back from the pub on a Friday night with two or three pints inside him.

She would smile as she sang the verses that David had romanced her with, even when they were middle-aged; tears would come to her eyes at the memory.

Ifan, his mother and twin brothers, Bryn and George, had returned to the valley to live with gran when he was five years old. His dad had been caught in a collapse in a mine and his mother Bronwyn could not stay in a place that held so many memories of him.

It was not just her memories, but fear for her older boys who had worshipped their father and planned on following him down the mines when they were old enough. She dreaded the thought of losing them too and decided that a move back to her home away from that possibility was the only way forward. But it was her youngest son who had worried her the most. He would barely eat and at night he would toss and turn in the grip of dark dreams that had him waking; crying and calling for her.

After a few months it became clear that Bryn and George were unhappy despite finding jobs on a local farm. A soon as they turned eighteen they had announced that they wanted to return to work in the mines. They found this rural farming community too quiet and they missed their friends from the cobbled, narrow streets of the mining town. Despite her misgivings, Bronwyn knew that she could not stop them from following their own paths because of her fear. After some failed attempts to get them to change their minds, she arranged for them to board with a neighbour in the same street that they had grown up in. Bronwyn had tried very hard to be brave for Ifan's sake as they stood hand in hand on the platform, watching the train leave the station carrying the boys back to South Wales.

That was three years ago and despite initially missing his brothers very much; they made an effort to write to him often, occasionally sending photographs and also ringing to speak to him on the old black telephone in the kitchen. Ifan was now ten years old and had taken on the role of man of the house. Life had settled into a happy and stable routine and he had flourished. His mother too had gone back to work part-time in nearby Dolgellau in a store, walking Ifan to school in the morning and waiting for him when the bell rang at the end of the day. They would arrive home to supper on the table and Ifan particularly loved his gran's homemade berry crumble and thick custard.

In the summer holidays after his mother finished work the three of them would take a picnic part of the way up the track that led to the summit of Cadair, sitting on the mossy grass as they ate egg sandwiches and sticky homemade ginger cake. Megan would tell stories of David's life as a shepherd and one story that Ifan loved to hear time and time again was about the black sheep.

One winter when unexpected early snow was deep on the ground, the farmer and David had trekked up the narrow path to find the flock and bring them down the mountain to safety. It was almost impossible to see through the still falling snow and they had almost given up hope of finding them when David had spotted the old matriarch of the flock. Black against the whiteness and surrounded by unmoving mounds that looked like snowdrifts. As soon as the black ewe saw the men she recognised, she bleated and headed towards them, followed by the rest of the flock; visible now as they turned their dark faces in their direction. Within an hour they were all safely down to the lower slopes and feeding on bales of hay hungrily.

What's in a Name?

Gran said that in these dangerous mountains every flock needed a strong black ewe at the heart of the flock; wherever she was, they would be safe.

Now gran was very sick and the doctor had been in twice today. Ifan sat rigidly in the delicate chair holding a fragile, blue veined hand in his own small grasp. He looked up at her lined and much loved face and held his breath as he saw her eyes flicker and then open.

'Hello Cariad my love,' Megan turned her head on the pillow and squeezed his hand lightly.

'Gran are you feeling better?' Ifan leaned forward over the patchwork quilt and stared intently into her deeply lined face.

'I am very tired pet, but so pleased to see you sitting there like a vision,' she swallowed with difficulty but then smiled at the worried looking child. 'Nothing that a good milky cup of cocoa wouldn't fix!'

The boy stood up and removed her hand from his, placing it gently across the quilt… He rushed to the kitchen where his mother was making supper and grabbed her arm.

'Mum, mum, gran's awake and says she wants a cup of milky cocoa.'

His mother frowned and pulling out a chair from the scrubbed wooden kitchen table, she gently pushed Ifan into the seat. Resting her hands on his thin shoulders she kissed the top of his head before leaving the room.

A few minutes later, Ifan heard sobbing coming from the big front bedroom and he rushed down the corridor and burst into the room. His mother was sat in the velvet chair holding Megan's hand up to her lips; tears filling her eyes. The boy went to the other side of the bed and looked down at his gran as she lay with her eyes closed and a slight smile on her lips. He looked across at Bronwyn and she met his gaze for a moment before shaking her head slowly from side to side.

What's in a Name?

A few days later the cottage was filled with mourners, most of whom had known Megan all her life and certainly since she had moved into the cottage with David Lloyd so many years ago. Ifan's brothers had returned home for the funeral and were now on the back porch drinking beer with the men from the town. Ifan slipped away to his gran's bedroom and sat in the velvet chair with his small fists clenched on his lap. Through his tears he looked over at the bedside table and saw Megan's reading glasses perched on top of a white envelope. He picked it up and saw that it was addressed to him. The letter was unsealed so he pulled back the flap and removed the slip of paper inside. He read the spidery writing that covered the small piece of paper.

Cariad, please do not be sad. I am in a wonderful place now with your granddad and I want you to remember the story of the black sheep on the mountain. Your mum is now the heart of the family and if you stay close to her and follow her you will be safe and happy. Be brave and I love you my lamb. Gran.

After the visitors had all left; his two brothers' and his mum sat around the kitchen table with a pot of tea talking about the day and exchanging memories of Megan. Ifan slipped away quietly and put himself to bed. For a few minutes he stared up at the ceiling above his head and then across at his album containing all the family photos he treasured. A white envelope protruded between the pages and there it would stay forever. He switched off the bedside light and within minutes he had drifted off to sleep, dreaming of a black sheep leading her flock across the green hillside in the sunshine.

JANE

The news of her pregnancy was a surprise to the 45 year old and to be honest not a welcome one. Her two other children, both boys in their late teens, were very happily studying at the same university fifty miles away. Whilst she missed them all the time, she had sailed through the empty-nest syndrome perfectly well.

Jane had gone to the doctor to enquire about hormone replacement as she seemed to have entered the menopause early. Before prescribing the treatment, her doctor felt it was a good idea to rule out any other reason for her symptoms with a simple test. He delivered the news with a certain amount of care to a bewildered Jane; sitting at her side with a glass of water and a box of tissues to hand.

He had known his patient for twenty-five years and was well aware that Jane was looking forward to some long-awaited overseas trips with her husband Mike and that the planned six weeks in Australia would now have to be put on the back burner. Jane took the glass of water and sat in dumbstruck silence for several minutes as the doctor waited patiently.

It was at that moment that she felt the 'surprise' kick gently against her hand clasped across her stomach. Obviously the baby was keen to voice its opinion about the matter and was making quite sure that she knew there were now two of them to consider.

Following a scan the following week it was determined that Jane was just over five months pregnant and what she had thought was middle-aged spread was going to be little more difficult to shift than anticipated. She had insisted that her husband, who was still in denial about the whole thing, come to the appointment and saw the look on his face as he watched his latest child squirm and kick on the monitor.

'Can you tell us what the sex is at this stage?' Jane gripped Mike's hand as he leaned forward to peer at the screen.

'I don't want to know Mike, please let's wait until it is born,' she smiled apologetically at the nurse who was just about to spill the beans.

Mike grumbled all the way home about how quick she had been to give away all the baby and toddler clothes, and did she know how much it was going to cost to buy all new kit including one of those new-fangled pushchairs?

'Darling,' Jane reached over and laid her hand on his knee. 'That was fifteen years ago and you never know; this baby might be a girl.'

He shrugged distractedly and Jane could see that Mike was not as invested in the turn of events as she already was. Of course he did not have the benefit of hormones racing through her system, which to be honest she rather enjoyed as she had thought they might have been totally dormant. Except of course after the office BBQ five months ago; she chuckled away to herself much to Mike's annoyance.

Thankfully they had not reached the stage of paying for their planned six weeks in Australia and Mike now moved his extended vacation time to early the next year so that he could be there for the arrival of the new addition. He tried to be enthusiastic about his impending fatherhood but it was a process he thought he would never experience again…

He loved his sons but admitted to himself that he enjoyed them a great deal more now that the three of them shared similar interests such as football and heading down the pub for a swift pint on Sunday lunchtimes. Now that they were enjoying university he had found himself excited about the prospect of increased freedom to pick up some of the old threads of his life. He had been looking forward to scaling back at his firm too and letting his partner take the slack so he and Jane could take those trips they had promised themselves. He thought back to the sleepless nights with two babies under three and then again when they hit their teens with less than fond memories.

However over the next few weeks he found himself looking over at Jane sitting on the sofa with her feet up on the coffee table, knitting baby booties and matinee jackets in soft white wool and did not have the heart to be disgruntled for long. In fact she was blooming and he had to admit the re-emergence of her hormones was doing wonders for his love life.

The next hurdle of course was to tell the boys… Dan and Geoff came home for the Christmas break; six weeks after their parents had received their unexpected news. Mike had picked them up from the station and they barrelled through the front door eager to see their mum and enjoy one of her home-cooked meals. They flung their bags on the carpet before turning to give her a hug. Both stopped in their tracks, looking at the obvious and now very noticeable bump that Jane was cradling with both hands.

Nervously Jane searched their faces and was highly surprised when they both fell about laughing.

'Great gag Mum,' Dan was hanging onto the door frame to the lounge. Geoff whipped out his mobile phone and insisted on taking a selfie with his head next to her bump whilst Jane and Mike looked at each other in bewilderment.

Mike put his hand on Geoff's shoulder and reached out his other to Dan who stopped laughing at the serious expression on his father's face.

What's in a Name?

'You are kidding, right!' Both of them stared at their parents before picking up their backpacks and heading silently up the stairs to their rooms.

Both boys had jobs over the Christmas break in bars in the centre of town and during the day they would help out around the house as Jane tired easily. Her ankles swelled and she found it difficult to focus on household chores and preparing meals. Mike took over the cooking and in the evening, when the boys were at work, they would sit on the sofa and she would rest her legs across his knees as he massaged her feet. She also became very tearful and the men in her life tiptoed around her in case they set her off again.

Mike spent as much time as possible with his sons over the holidays trying to persuade them that having a baby brother would be cool; they would be able to teach him how to play football and about girls. The three of them convinced themselves that it would most likely be a boy, especially as there had not been a girl in either side of the family since Jane had been born into a family of five brothers.

After a subdued Christmas Day with a rather crispy turkey and soggy potatoes cooked by father and sons; the more urgent business of preparing for the new arrival took priority.

Mike had decorated the nursery and he and the boys had managed to assemble the cot and various essential pieces of furniture before Dan and Geoff returned to university in the middle of January. Early in February he and Jane had gone to the large industrial park to one of the large stores that sold pushchairs and car seats and were both exhausted by the time they reached home. Mike had not been to the pub for several weeks and seeing that he was looking frazzled, Jane told him to meet his friends for a drink whilst she caught up on one of her weekly television shows. She assured him that she would be fine for an hour and reluctantly he headed off patting his phone in his back pocket.

His friends, who were the same age as Mike, gave him a hard time in a good-natured way and promised to turn out for the school football matches to offer moral support when the other kids called him granddad. They then sat smugly back with their pints and reminisced about sleepless nights and nappies.

Halfway through the programme; Jane felt the first twinges and ignored them as indigestion. By the time the next adverts rolled around there was no doubt that something was definitely happening. She grabbed her mobile phone and dialled Mike's number holding her breath as another pain rippled across her abdomen.

The next morning Dan and Geoff arrived at the hospital and were directed to the maternity ward waiting room. After a few minutes their father came in still dressed in his green gown and hugged them one after the other. He looked shattered and as he stared at them tears rolled down his cheeks.

'Dad for god's sake where's mum and what's happened?' Dan grabbed Mike's arm shocked and terrified what the answer might be.

Unable to speak Mike gestured for them to follow him and they walked behind him glancing at each other nervously.

Their father pushed open the door to the labour suite where they saw their mum, flushed and exhausted but smiling down at a bundle in her arms. Mike walked across and placed his arm around Jane's shoulders looking lovingly down at the two of them.

The boys felt reassured by their mother's smile and she beckoned them to the other side of the bed. From here they could see the scrunched up face of their new little brother and they both reached out to gently touch the blanket he was wrapped in. At their touch the baby opened his eyes and it seemed as though he was looking directly at them. They caught their breath and knew immediately that they would move heaven and earth for this little boy.

Jane glanced at Mike and they both smiled and then she turned to her two sons. 'Meet your sister Lucy boys.'

Dan and Geoff looked at each other in disbelief and then Geoff touched his mum's shoulder gently as he leant over to take one tiny hand in his.

'Great gag mum…'

JACK

The gardens of the old house were kept immaculately by a team of unseen gardeners, so that others may visit to walk its paths, and smell the fragrances that drift like smoke through the air.

However, not everyone is allowed to wander unaccompanied across the green and luscious lawns, to discover hidden treasures behind evergreen bushes and ancient trees. This privilege is only for those, who in their lives have touched plants with love and respect. No ripping of the roots from the soil or unworthy cuts with sharpened tools when the blooms have faded and died; just a gentle touch prompted by love.

One such special visitor to the magic garden was an elderly man who walked delightedly amongst the riotous late spring colours of the flower beds and along the old stone paths. His name was Jack and he had spent a lifetime working in his own garden; gifting that love of the earth and all that grew within it to his three children and many grandchildren. As he walked in the soft late spring sunlight he caught sight of a flash of pink behind an old wooden shed and heard the tinkle of childish laughter. Intrigued he made his way across the dew damp grass to explore further.

His hand reached out and touched the delicate petals of the wall climbing rose and it reminded Jack of his two daughters. The plant was beautiful and vibrant; with the strength to grow and bloom every year in this hidden spot of the garden. He remembered how delighted Katherine and Amelia had been when Jack had bought them their first climbing rose to grace the wall of their home. He smiled to himself as he remembered the looks on their faces every time he arrived home with a new pot from the nursery on his way home from work. When their mother has died when they were still so young it had been a way of bringing light back into their desolate home.

As he breathed in the scent of the pink blossoms an image came to her mind of a beautiful woman sat in a chair holding her beloved children closely. A feeling of joy spread through him and he stood for a moment relishing this precious memory.

This garden was not a formal place of worship but that did not matter as he knew that there was spirituality in simple things. Such as being amongst these beautiful plants and listening to the insects that hummed with the joy of spring. It was also in the sharing of fairy stories and cocoa before bedtime, hearing his children's laughter and knowing that he was fulfilling his dying wife's last wishes.

Part of that wish was that he continued to create a special garden for her daughters and son. She wanted them to grow to adulthood appreciating the beauty of nature and how to treat growing things with love and tenderness. It was a task that at first had been very painful but over the years it became a source of joy for all of them and to those that they welcomed into their home. Many a stray dog or cat found sanctuary amongst the bushes and flowers along the borders of the lawn and even the wild foxes knew they could bring their young in safety.

Jack continued to wander, touching a rose here and a gentle scented lilac there. A yellow rose caught his eye as it was the only bloom of that colour in the garden. It stood out amongst the pale pinks and vibrant reds and he thought of his son Andrew standing proudly between his two sisters and smiled to himself at the memory.

What's in a Name?

He found a stone seat under a shady tree surrounded by funny little statues of dwarf musicians. He fancied he heard teenage laughter and was that really the sound of a guitar playing nearby? Peacefully he sat drinking in the scene before him until a flash of colour startled him. Hovering before him was a delicate butterfly decked out in vibrant gold and shimmering green. Amazed, Jack held out his hand and the little creature settled delicately into his palm. They looked at each other for a moment or two and then the butterfly flew away back towards an old magnolia tree.

No words had been spoken but a message had been passed between them. Jack knew that he would be welcome to visit the garden anytime that he wished; a place to remember those that he had cherished and to touch again plants and petals he had loved. But for now it was time to leave. With a lingering look at the beauty that surrounded him, he walked across the grass dotted with daisies and faded from sight into the walls of the boarded up house.

Volume II

About Volume II

Our legacy is not always about money or fame, but rather in the way that people remember our name after we have gone. In these sixteen short stories we discover the reasons why special men and women will stay in the hearts and minds of those who have met them. Romance, revenge and sacrifice all play their part in the lives of these characters.

Kenneth watches the love of his life dance on New Year's Eve while Lily plants very special flowers every spring for her father. Martha helps out a work colleague as Norman steps back out into the world to make a difference. Owen brings light into a house and Patrick risks his life in the skies over Britain and holds back from telling a beautiful redhead that he loves her.

Meet Queenie and Rosemary who have both lost their husbands and must face a very different future. One that will take courage and the use of new technology.

Sonia is an entitled princess whose father has reached the end of his tether and Theresa has to deal with a bully in the checkout. Usher is an arrogant narcissist with a docile wife and is used to getting his own way and Vanessa worries about the future of her relationship with her teenage son.

Walter is a loner and is happy with just his dog for company, Xenia is the long awaited first baby of a young couple. Yves is a dashing romeo who has the tables turned on him unexpectedly and Zoe… Well she can see into the future.

In one way or another all these characters will be remembered by those whose lives they have touched.

KENNETH

Kenneth Fitzgerald looked across the crowded ballroom at the woman that he had loved for a lifetime.

Georgina was surrounded by attentive male admirers, and was holding court as she always did, with elegance and grace. He watched as she tilted her head to one side to listen to the young man sitting next to her, cupping her hand delicately behind her ear, to better hear his comments over the sound of the band.

The handsome companion was her grandson Timothy, and even at first glance you could see the resemblance; the same blue eyes, golden hair colour and a long refined nose. Georgie was 90 years old and yet her beauty was undiminished. Kenneth knew he was biased. He remembered his stunned reaction to meeting her for the first time over 70 years ago, in this same ballroom on New Year's Eve 1935.

Georgina Crowley was the daughter of a millionaire financier who had managed to survive the Wall Street crash in 1929, by converting his wealth in previous years, into a renowned art collection. Malcolm Crowley was an astute businessman and had never squandered his money on the trappings of wealth. He had also salted away cash and jewellery on his various international travels, providing a comfortable buffer for the family, and those that had worked for him loyally over the last thirty years.

He was as canny with his three children as he was with his wealth. His two sons had followed him into the firm after studying for business degrees, and Georgina had also been encouraged to go to college, where she was now training to be a teacher. Malcolm firmly believed that all his children should have skills that could support them, should the financial climate not improve significantly in his lifetime. That is not to say that his youngest child did not also enjoy the benefits of being part of a wealthy family. Georgina was known to have exquisite taste, and her slim figure was the perfect shape to model the latest fashions. To be fair, many of the designs were copied from the leading fashion magazines, and recreated on her treasured Singer sewing machine

Kenneth brought himself back to the present and felt his heart pounding in his chest. It was the same every year, when he remembered that first New Year's Eve, when he had fallen madly in love at first sight with Georgina Crowley. It had not been a one-sided infatuation, and at that first touch of her delicate hand in his own, he had felt a tremor that caused him to look up into her face. Her pink lips had parted in surprise and her smile dazzled him.

They had danced all night circling the floor; perfectly matched in their love of the foxtrot and quickstep. The other party goers had moved to one side to watch this golden couple as they seamlessly moved from one dance to another, and Malcolm Crowley paused in his discussions with a group of men, to watch his daughter's delight in this young man's embrace.

Kenneth had wanted to kiss those pink lips at midnight but was aware of the scrutiny from those around them. He had whispered in Georgina's ear as they waltzed to the final tune of the old year.

'Shall we slip away at midnight and find some moon and starlight?'

She had looked into his eyes and smiled, nodding her head in agreement.

As the clock struck midnight, Georgina rushed to her parents at their table and kissed and hugged them both. In the ensuing rush as the other guests did likewise, the two of them had slipped out of the large double doors at the end of the ballroom and Kenneth had guided her to his car parked along the drive. He grabbed a blanket from the back seat of the roadster and placed it around Georgina's shoulders before helping her into the front seat. He raced around to the other side of the car and within minutes they were roaring down the hill from the house into the dark night.

Kenneth drove carefully as the road was slick with ice and he was aware that he was responsible for a very precious cargo. Although it was a cold night he knew just the place to take Georgina on this magical occasion. A spot high above the city, where the lights and sounds of New Year's Eve would provide a backdrop for their first kiss.

He looked across at Georgina as she clasped the plaid blanket around her bare shoulders, and smiled at her obvious delight at this adventure. His eyes were only off the road for seconds, but it was still long enough for him to miss the broken down car around a curve in the road.

He regained consciousness and raised his hand to his forehead; it came away wet and sticky. He wiped blood from his eyes and tried to move his body. Finally he was able to push himself into a sitting position against the upturned roadster and he desperately looked for Georgina. The moon came out from behind a cloud and he took a sharp intake of breath as he saw her crumpled form by the rear bumper of the car. He crawled across and managed to pull her crushed and lifeless body into his arms… his heart was pounding in his chest and he tried to wake her by touching her face and calling her name. After several minutes he rested his head back against the car and he knew that she was gone.

'Please, please do not take her ... it is my fault and it should be me... take me... please take me and save her.'

On New Year's Day, Georgie asked her youngest grandson to drive her to the cemetery. She came here often to visit her husband's grave. Phillip had been a wonderful man and she had grown to love him during the long summer of 1942. They had twin sons born in 1944 but tragically Phillip had been killed in the last weeks of the war. He had been brought home and buried in the Crowley family plot close by her house and their sons. She still missed his loving kindness. However, she admitted to herself that it was a different kind of love to the one that has swept her off her feet that magical New Year's Eve in 1935.

Whilst her grandson watched from the car, Georgina spent some minutes at Phillip's monument. Then walking carefully, leaning on her stick, she moved down the icy path until she stopped before another gravestone. Tears gathered in her pale blue eyes as she read the inscription.

Kenneth Fitzgerald
Beloved son and brother.
1910–1935
Killed in an automobile accident.

It was 70 years ago, and yet every New Year's Day, Georgie relived those dreadful first moments when she had woken in the hospital. She had a dreadful headache but thankfully didn't seem to have any other major injuries. Her mother and father were sitting by her bedside and Malcolm gently took her hand in his. Her first words were asking for Kenneth, and she still remembered the look of anguish on her father's face as he braced himself to tell her the news.

She touched the top of the headstone and smiled to herself. He had been there again last night at the family ball, watching from the shadows as he had done every year, and she had felt that same giddy feeling as that first New Year's Eve. She suspected that this time however it was more likely that her medication was no longer effective in keeping her failing heart beating.

She felt a touch on her shoulder and looked up into the smiling face of her grandson.

'Time to go Gran… It is getting cold and I need to get you back home.'

Georgie took his arm and they moved carefully up the path. She turned for one last look at Kenneth's grave.

She whispered to herself. 'Next year my love, next year we will dance again on New Year's Eve.'

LILY

Lily dusted off her hands. They had been covered in soil from planting the three little primulas that she and her mother had picked up at the nursery today. Her mother always let Lily pick the colours and this year the purple petals with their golden centres danced in the soft evening breeze. She picked up her small watering can and gently moistened around the base of the plants like her mum had shown her.

'There you go Daddy, I promise to look after them all summer, watering them every day and picking off the dead flowers to let others grow like mum showed me.'

It was Easter and tomorrow, Lily and her little brother Owen would race around the house looking for the small cream eggs that her mother had bought at the supermarket yesterday. Both of them were very excited and it was really the first year that her brother understood what the egg hunt was all about. Mum said that three each was more than enough especially as they were going to the dentist soon for a check-up.

However, the real prize was the two large chocolate eggs that were hidden in very special places. In her father's wardrobe perhaps, or his study where he would read them a story before they went up to bed, or even the garden shed that her mum laughingly called his man cave.

The next day Lily and Owen got up early and began searching the house. It took them an hour to find the six small creamy eggs and by the time they had rushed into the kitchen to show off their finds, two of them had already been eaten.

What's in a Name?

Their mother looked at the smeared evidence of their successful hunt around their mouths and took the remainder off them for later.

'You need to eat your breakfast and then you can find the other eggs, I am going to hide them now so no peeking.'

The children hurriedly ate their bowls of cereal and drank their juice eager to get on with the hunt. After about ten minutes their mother returned to the kitchen and clapped her hands.

'Okay, let's see how quickly you can find the big prizes.'

Lily took their dishes to the sink and the two children ran off hand in hand heading for their father's study to continue the search.

They found one egg after about five minutes. It was beneath the big oak desk in a waste basket hidden by some crumpled paper. There was a card attached to the egg with 'Owen' written in big letters and he clasped the colourful box in his small hands as they raced from one room to the other. Finally they gave up on the house and headed out to the garden shed. There hidden under a cloth in a large plant pot sat a beautiful egg nestled in its packaging with a note perched beside it.

'The flowers are beautiful Lily and your daddy's favourite colours.'

From the kitchen window their mother saw her nine year old daughter lead her brother up the path to the house. Owen was clasping his egg to his chest and beaming from ear to ear. Lily looked up as they entered the kitchen and smiled gently at her mother as a look of understanding passed between them.

That night Lily placed the egg on her bedside cabinet next to the photograph of her daddy in his army uniform surrounded by other men in his team. He was smiling and

What's in a Name?

looked happy. It was the last picture taken of him two years ago and Lily stared at it for a long time before switching off her light.

Tomorrow the Easter egg would join the other one on the shelf in her wardrobe and would never be eaten.

MARTHA

Jennifer stood in the middle of the lift and stared at her black leather pumps. She noticed a scuff on the left side of the toe of the right shoe, realising that she had kicked the full waste basket a little harder than she thought at the time. She was weary and unusually tearful. It had been a tough week all round with particularly hard advertising revenue to achieve, but it had ended on the sourest note of all.

She managed a team of fifty telephone sales canvassers who sold high end car and luxury property advertising for the national online paper she worked for. These days both those markets were tough going.

It seemed that people were hanging onto high ticket items waiting for a rise in demand for both.

However, her boss who lived in his ivory tower of an office on the top floor of the building; still insisted on increasing her targets for revenue on a monthly basis, dismissive about the state of the market. Despite creative campaigns and offers, she was finding it more and more difficult to satisfy his demands.

Her guys worked their socks off and she knew that they did so for their generous salaries and commission. She also knew that they did their very best to achieve the targets that she asked of them, even though they might groan when she wrote them on their sales board in the office. When they hit their daily and weekly revenues, they always included her in their trip to the pub for a celebratory pint, and on tough days, most would stay late to pick up an extra car or property advert to make up the numbers.

The doors to the lift opened and she wearily made her way across the cement floor to where her company car was parked. She had to admit that she could not complain about her hybrid Turing which was a perk given to sales managers once they had been in the job for five years or longer. She had inherited the vehicle from one of the senior executives when he retired a month ago and she loved all its special add on features and programming. At this very moment it was about the only thing about the job apart from her team that she did love.

She saw that the car was already idling and that there was the faint sound of music coming from the open passenger side window. She smiled and knew that the day was just about to get a little better. She touched the keypad in her hand and the boot lid opened so she could store her briefcase away. She went around to the driver's side and slid into the leather seat and rested her head back against the comforting upholstery.

'Bad day love?' The calming tones of the other occupant of the car made her open her eyes.

'The worst Martha, the worst.' Jennifer reached across and turned the music down a notch. 'Beaumont came into the office before everyone left, and gave us his usual Friday afternoon lecture about how we were not achieving our targets, and that the team were obviously neither motivated nor managed well enough to do the job.'

She paused as her eyes welled up with more tears and sat silently for a moment. 'He then turned to me and told me to be in his office first thing Monday morning and then stormed out.'

As she bit her lip, she felt warm lightly scented air move across her face and body calming her down. She wiped her eyes and blew her nose before pushing the buttons on her pathfinder to take them home.

What's in a Name?

As the car exited the underground garage she checked right and left before nudging the accelerator to join the line of traffic headed in the direction out of the city. She switched the car to auto but kept her hands lightly on the wheel.

'That was most unfair of him Jennifer and very unprofessional,' Martha spoke quietly in her ear. 'That is a deliberate tactic to make you worry all weekend about your job and your team's security and my advice is to put it out of your mind completely however hard that might be.'

'I know Martha,' Jennifer kept an eye on the busy Friday evening traffic at the same time as acknowledging the truth of her companion's words.

'This car and your unexpected friendship are about the only thing keeping me in the job at the moment,' she smiled ruefully. 'Of course that is not entirely true, I love my team and I can't bear the thought of them being left in the hands of that narcissistic jumped up jerk.'

'I may have done something that should help.'

Without taking her eyes off the road, Jennifer stiffened with surprise. Martha would never do anything against the rules; she was by nature very rigid and predictable and this was a complete shock.

'What are you talking about Martha, what have you done?'

There was a moment's pause. 'As system administrator, I have access to the emails sent throughout the company, and I read Beaumont's this morning. I found several from the chairman of the board of directors insisting that he had to cut at least £200,000 from this year's staff budget.'

Shocked and now even more worried, Jennifer gripped the steering wheel; despite having no need to except in an emergency. 'Oh no Martha, if they find out they will terminate you.'

Martha continued. 'Well actually I am afraid I did a little more than that.'

'Oh my friend that is so dangerous. I don't want anything to happen to you because of my problems.'

'Don't worry; Beaumont will be in no position to do anything to me or to you and your team by Monday morning.'

This was serious, and seeing a gap in the parked cars to her left, Jennifer indicated and pulled in. Now she could focus on what her friend was saying.

'Tell me everything Martha and don't leave anything out.'

'I replied to the chairman's emails on Beaumont's behalf after he left this evening, resigning effective immediately. His reasoning being that he is paid £250,000 per year plus various benefits that amounted to over £400,000. He stated that this would prevent any need for a staffing reduction for the next two years, enabling the market to improve and also current sales targets to remain in place. He also recommended that you become Sales Director with a salary increase and that you be given the freedom to manage your team as you see fit to achieve those targets.'

Jennifer found it difficult to take this all in and was absolutely speechless that this mild mannered entity, who only wished everyone well, should have come up with such a Machiavellian plan.

'But Martha, they will simply refuse to accept his resignation and worse still they might investigate his email and find out you tampered with it.'

'Jennifer I designed the system and know how to cover my tracks very well. I also took out a little insurance policy that will encourage the board to accept his resignation without question.'

This was now becoming surreal and Jennifer shook her head from side to side in amazement.

What's in a Name?

'I'm waiting Martha…don't keep me in suspense.'

'I checked Beaumont's personal text messages on his company phone and discovered that he has been having an affair with the head of human resources; who is also married incidentally. Unfortunately one of those texts will arrive on the Chairman's phone by the time he gets his first cup of coffee on his desk on Monday. A scandal at the moment is the last thing the company needs; Beaumont's resignation will be seen as a blessing.

Jennifer was finding it very difficult to get her head around this seemingly well thought out solution to her dilemma, but then realised that it was already underway, and nothing that she could do at this point could change that.

Making sure that she was clear to join the decreasing traffic out of the city she instructed the car to indicate and proceed homeward. She rested her hands lightly on the steering wheel as it made necessary slight adjustments.

'Please say you are not angry with me.' Martha sounded contrite and Jennifer took a deep breath. 'No, I am not angry with you Martha, although you have overstepped the bounds of your job specification. I know it was done because you're my friend.' She paused and tried to be as clear as possible.

'You must never put yourself in danger of termination like this again. Please promise me that they will never discover how involved you have become with me and my team. We rely on your essential assistance to help us achieve those major targets week after week.'

As the car entered the drive to Jennifer's home, and before she switched off the ignition she waited for a response. 'I promise Jennifer.'

The front door opened and her husband stood in the doorway framed by the light from the hall. Jennifer retrieved

What's in a Name?

her briefcase from the back of the car and walked into his comforting embrace.

'How was your day love, did you end the week better than it started.' James looked down at his wife.

She smiled at him and they wandered arm and arm into the kitchen where a delicious aroma filled the air.

'You are not going to believe this, but you know that our system administrator is the latest A.I. technology called Martha… well it seems that she is a little more intelligent than we expected!

NORMAN

Norman carried his plate carefully across to the gingham covered table under the window, setting it down next to his cup of tea that had been as carefully transported a few minutes before. He could not walk without his stick and had to adapt his routine to fit around this inconvenience. He steadied himself on the back of the wooden chair and deposited his walking aid up against the window sill. He turned himself around and sat down heavily with a sigh of relief.

He assaulted the still steaming cup of tea with four spoons of sugar and smiled wryly at the silence that accompanied this act of rebellion. If Ruby had been sitting opposite him there would have been hell to pay. He closed his eyes and willed the disobedient tear to cease its descent down his cheek. He sniffed and reached for the butter.

His flat was in an anonymous looking block on a small estate that had been built in the 1990s. He had moved here begrudgingly from their little terrace house that had been home for fifty years. The council were going to knock the late Victorian homes down and make way for a modern housing project. As a widower without any living family, he did not qualify for one of the new three-bedroomed semi-detached houses. They had moved his bits of furniture and treasured belongings to the flat, but the money that they paid him for the compulsory purchase of the house was still sitting in a bank account untouched.

He managed his simple needs on his state and army pension, only glancing briefly at the monthly statements that showed a steadily increasing balance, before throwing them in a drawer in the sideboard.

There had been an effort by his previous neighbours to fight the compulsory purchase. He had watched the protests in the street dispassionately, ignoring the knocks on his door from those soliciting his support. Ruby had only just died and a part of him had as well. He had been numb at the time and also strangely voiceless but he had looked upon the resultant pay out as blood money. As he looked around the small room that had never seen a visitor, he realised how much he had relied on Ruby and the community spirit in his old neighbourhood.

Norman's flat was on the second floor of the building and thankfully the lift was in operation most of the time. He couldn't manage the one flight of stairs now even with the stick; resenting this as evidence of his further decline. During the day the building had always been reasonably quiet and he barely noticed the passing of the hours. That is until he would hear the sound of the children returning from school and diving straight into the playground at the front of the flats. He usually opened his windows and sat with a cup of tea, enjoying their shrieks and laughter. It reminded him of his own dead son when he was that age; long before he joined the army and went to Iraq.

Recently however there had been new sounds and they drowned out the childish laughter. Teenagers from a neighbouring estate were prowling the stairwells and communal areas of the blocks nearest to them, but away from family and possible consequences in their own neighbourhood. His own block had taken on a seedy and unwholesome appearance with evidence of night-time drinking and drug taking on the landings and underground garage. The local residence association had contacted the police and there had been a

What's in a Name?

begrudging response which included one or two more cars patrolling at night, but no arrests were made. The council representative had said that they were powerless to provide security with cutbacks to essential services already.

The residents now rarely went out at night unless absolutely necessary; locking their doors and windows and turning their televisions up louder to cover the noises of anarchy on their doorstep. Children no longer played on the swings as aggressive teenagers of both genders took over the playground in the central area as a gathering point in the afternoons, jobless and bored. Graffiti began to spread across the walls of the ground floor and up the stairs; Norman shook his head at the hatred and violence it depicted. He had never felt so powerless in his life.

It was Wednesday and Norman always went down to the legion for a pint and bite of lunch. It was his only interaction with others during the week, except for the cashiers at the local supermarket. He laid out his suit on the bed and found a shirt that was crisply ironed. He would wear his regimental tie today and give his black shoes an extra polish. He needed to look his best for what lay ahead.

An hour later he made his way through the swing doors of the legion and walked past the walls covered with photographs of those who had served and passed away. One day his image would join them and younger men would mentally salute him as they walked into the bar. But he was not there yet, and grasping his stick firmly, he straightened his back and walked briskly through the tables of men talking quietly in this place that linked them to their years of service. Some looked up and said… 'Morning Sergeant Major.'

He acknowledged them silently with a nod.

'Atten… Shun'

At the barked command thirty pairs of eyes swivelled to the front of the room and automatically several stood to attention.

As Norman's stern gaze descended on the other men, they too stood to join their comrades.

'You have all served your country bravely, but now you, like me sit silently by and watch as an enemy infiltrates our way of life. The people we fought for are under attack and barricaded into their homes afraid to breathe in the fresh air and walk unmolested.'

Several men nodded and Norman could read their body language as he had thousands of soldiers before. They too had lost their purpose and it was time to give them their pride back.

Later that afternoon the children arrived home from school and were ushered straight into their flats on the different levels of the apartment block. A few stray elderly residents also made their way back from shopping and packed into the lifts that would distribute them over several floors. The block was preparing for the daily invasion of the gang.

They were not disappointed, and as the warm sun hit the playground it began to fill with the dross from the neighbouring estate, laughing and throwing their rubbish on the ground. When dusk fell they would start working their way through the block with their spray paints and drug paraphernalia; turning this community into a no go area for decent people.

Suddenly one the group caught sight of movement coming from the direction of the main road. He shushed his mates and one by one they went silent. They watched as an old man walking with a stick marched up the street with determination. He was followed by at least thirty men in rows, also marching in time. They wore suits and looked proudly to the front where their leader preceded them. Some of the youths began pointing and laughing but a tall, older boy told them to be quiet.

What's in a Name?

The marching men arrived in front of the block of flats and turned sharply to face the playground. Norman took three steps closer and placed both his hands over the head of his stick. He looked to his right as two large vans marked with the name of an industrial cleaning company pulled up to the kerb.

He turned and addressed the youths now waiting expectantly and looking at each other in stunned silence.

'These men behind me have fought in wars around the world and are all trained killers. They will now be patrolling our estate day and night in teams of three and have orders to treat any they find defacing the walls, using drugs or threatening the residents as terrorists which is what you are.'

Norman paused and behind him he heard the snap of boots on the road surface as a number of the men took three steps forward and stood with their arms folded menacingly.

Sergeant Major Norman Smith pointed at the two vans. 'These contractors will now clean the graffiti off the walls and remove your filth from the stairs and hallways. You will now pick up all your rubbish you have dropped and put it into the bins provided. You will then leave this estate and not return again. These men behind me are just a handful of those at my disposal and any ideas you might have of bringing reinforcements to assist you will be met with severe repercussions.'

The youth who the others followed, looked at the old man and smiled slightly as he shook his head. He pointed to the others to pick up their discarded cartons and soda bottles, which they did reluctantly. He glared at some and gave others a sharp word. He knew there were other soft targets out there. Perhaps not as convenient to his estate, but this one was no longer worth the hassle. Hoods up and hands in pockets, the youths turned and began to saunter nonchalantly out of the far exit of the playground.

What's in a Name?

As they did so Norman heard doors begin to open on the sunlit walkways behind him and voices as people tried to find out what was going on. He glanced behind him as the cleaning crews began unloading equipment from the back of the vans. He had finally found something to use that blood money for in a way that he could live with.

Applause broke out on the walkways, and as the last of the youths sauntered off down the road, a mother ventured out of the safety of the building holding her two children's hands. They broke away from her and raced into the playground shouting and laughing.

Soon others left the surrounding blocks and came to speak to Norman and their new protectors. As he watched the exchanges between the former soldiers and the liberated residents he saw how they carried themselves now with pride and purpose.

It was good to be back on the front line again.

OWEN

The old woman sat in the armchair in the dark. There was no need for light as she was blind. The disease had slowly eroded her vision, and then on a day when sun streamed through the open curtains; she lost sight of all that she loved.

She could hear her daughter Mary; clattering around in the kitchen preparing the tea tray with the best cups and a fresh baked chocolate sponge. The day had finally arrived when she would meet her great-grandson Owen. Her oldest daughter had gone to Australia forty years ago and she and her family lived in Sydney. Jennifer had returned a number of times to the UK, and on the last visit five years ago, she had brought a photograph of the youngest member of the family, four year old Owen, which was put in a silver frame on the mantelpiece.

Her eyesight was deteriorating at that time but she had managed to trace the lines of his dear little face with her fingers and smiled at the resemblance to her late husband Cliff. That same quirky grin and sparkling blue eyes that brought back such bittersweet memories.

Even though she could no longer see the photograph, the image remained in her mind and on winter days when the wind howled about the house, she imagined him on the beach near his home building sand castles.

The doorbell chimed and she listened as her daughter raced to the front door. There was laughter and exclamations of welcome and she imagined the crowded hall filled with her family. She tensed in the chair and held her breath as the door to the sitting room was flung open and she heard the click of the light switch.

'Mum, they're here,' Mary announced excitedly.

She felt movement close to her and a faint smell of chocolate as a small warm hand clasped her own. She breathed out and smiled as she turned in towards the warmth of the cheek against her skin.

'Hello Granny, I'm Owen,' the strong young voice declared.

'How do you do Owen,' tears bathed her sightless eyes. 'I have waited so long to meet you in person.'

Gently Owen took her hands, placing them side by side on his forehead. As she felt the springy curls under her fingers; small hands guided her palms down and across her great-grandson's face.

She laughed as she touched the widely spaced eye-brows, the gentle swell of eyelids with the fluttering of their lashes. Beneath her fingers she traced the contours of the boy's nose and recognised the shape as one belonging to Cliff. She continued down over the full lips and cupped the slightly squared chin in her left hand whilst placing her right over his beating heart.

The boy laughed delightedly and she smiled at the sound.

'Now you have seen me in 3D Granny… do you recognise me?'

PATRICK

The first time Patrick Walsh saw her, was as he wended his way slowly down the hill between the slow moving trucks on his motorbike. The road was lined with women and old men who were handing out hastily cut sandwiches and mugs of tea to the men in the trucks, whose outstretched hands gratefully received these simple acts of kindness. It was clear from the their faces that they found the peaceful summer skies overhead, and clamour of women's voices, a much needed reminder of home and safety.

He knew where they had come from, as for the last six days he had been flying over them as they had scrambled into small boats to be ferried out to the larger naval vessels waiting to take them to safety. He and his squadron were a part of the massive air defence operation. Thousands of soldiers were pouring off the beaches having gathered over the last few days from the surrounding countryside; exposed and being attacked by superior German forces. On the last run today his spitfire had received a direct hit to the cockpit from a persistent Messerschmitt Me 109; luckily missing his head by inches apart from a cut over his eye, earning him a few hours respite. His plane would be ready to fly first thing in the morning. The ground crews at all fighter squadrons were working around the clock to get pilots back in the air until the evacuation from the French coast was complete.

As he carefully manoeuvred between the trucks he responded to the shouts from the men above him with a small wave. He knew that their good natured jibes were aimed at

What's in a Name?

his uniform and the wings that it displayed, and that their friendly ribbing was their way of showing gratitude. He decided that it would be easier to wait until the convoy had passed to continue into the village square. He dismounted, standing by the hedge to watch the villagers as they persisted in their need to comfort these dispirited men with tea and offerings of food.

She stood out from the crowd of women. Tall with long red hair tied back with an emerald green ribbon, she was dressed in overalls and wore heavy boots. She had a natural elegance as she darted between an older woman, holding a tea tray piled with jam sandwiches, and the trucks. Despite the men's exhaustion, eager hands grasped the food, winking and flirting with the prettiest thing they had seen for a long while.

Patrick leaned back against the saddle of his bike and let himself enjoy this brief moment of humanity that was so rare today. He had been flying since the first weeks of the war and his squadron had suffered huge losses; particularly in the last few weeks as they had provided air cover for the retreating British forces.

They had been warned that far worse was to come as the enemy amassed both fighters and bombers for an all-out offensive on the country. Having already lost many friends, Patrick knew that it was only a matter of time before he became a statistic.

Some of his fellow pilots and aircrew decided that they would live as hard as they fought. There were plenty of pretty girls around the station that were delighted to dance the night away and bring some laughter and sometimes love into the young men's lives. He had seen the results of these whirlwind romances at the Saturday night dance in the village hall. As the airmen arrived in an ever changing group of young men,

What's in a Name?

expectant faces would be watching the door and it was not unusual to see a girl being led away in tears by her friends.

Patrick loved to dance but gently refused the invitations to take to the floor and over the last few months he had become regarded as something of a misery. His friends gave up on their attempts to persuade him that he should live for the moment, and with a wry smile he listened to the chat up lines that were guaranteed to pull the heartstrings of a pretty girl.

But now as he watched the red head flying back and forth and smiling up at the men in the trucks, he felt an overwhelming urge to hold her in his arms and waltz around a dance floor. He shook his head and reminded himself that it would only lead to heartbreak for her, and he couldn't bear the thought of those beautiful green eyes filling with tears.

An hour later the last truck in the convoy disappeared through the village square and out of sight. There would be more coming through from the coast, and Patrick watched as the crowd of villagers gathered up their cups and trays and disappeared back into their homes. They would prepare more from their meagre rations for the next wave of returning soldiers and be waiting for them by the roadside. He remained by the hedge until the red headed girl had linked arms with her mother and entered her house before riding down to the square.

'Patrick, are you awake my friend?' The voice of his Polish friend Jakub intruded into his daydream about dancing with his stunning red head.

'Just about, do you want to go to the Black Swan for a beer? He sat up and rested his head in his hands and tried to bring his mind back to reality.

He looked around the Nissen hut that was their home, taking in the four empty cots that waited for the new arrivals. They would be mostly teenagers with only a few hours flying solo, and none of them in combat. He was only twenty-four, but he felt like an old man compared to the fresh faced and eager boys that would come through that door tomorrow.

It was now August and the skies were filled with formations of enemy bombers most nights. His plane was grounded again having the undercarriage repaired after a problem on his last landing. His mechanic said he had the 'luck of the Irish'. Patrick was well aware that he was now one of only a handful of pilots remaining from the original group a year ago; he knew that his luck was bound to run out sooner or later.

There was just one thing that he needed tonight, and that was the sight of Red, and she would be helping out her dad behind the bar at the Black Swan.

Two hours later he and Jakub sat quietly at a corner table with their glasses of beer. One beer was the limit as both of them would be back in the skies tomorrow; a cockpit was no place for lack of concentration.

Jakub was married and expecting his first child and was happy to sit quietly in the warm and welcoming atmosphere thinking about his next leave in a week's time. Patrick however spent his time watching Red as she served customers and laughed with the regulars. That laugh was in his head and was added to all the other pieces of her that he carried with him as he flew missions. The thought of those green eyes helped dispel the voice of the other constant companion that was by his side each time he buckled himself into the cockpit. Her presence in his heart and mind had helped him control his fear; bringing the realisation that he was experiencing the very emotion he had desperately wanted to avoid; he was in love.

Over the weeks since that first day on the hill, there had been moments in the pub, when he would catch her eye and they would both smile then look away. By sitting at the bar when he popped in alone, he had gathered more information

What's in a Name?

about her. She wasn't called Red of course, but Margaret and Maggie to her friends. She didn't seem to have a boyfriend amongst the regulars who frequented the pub, and one day he overheard that she had been engaged to a soldier who had been killed within weeks of the war starting.

He would watch as she gently refused all attempts by eager young warriors to take her on a date, realising that her heart had already been broken. This reinforced his resolve not to give in to the growing need to tell Maggie of his feelings; convinced it would only bring her further sorrow.

Through the rest of the summer months missions intensified, with both daylight and night bombing raids on the docks and major cities; almost bringing the country to its knees. In the October the tide began to turn, but not without the loss of thousands of fighter pilots and bomber air crews. It was then that Patrick's luck ran out as he limped home with a badly damaged plane and shrapnel injuries in his chest and arm.

Patrick fought to stay conscious as the plane shuddered and bucked as he flew using his one good hand. Blood from a head wound almost blinded him, but as he saw the runway rushing up to meet him, he managed to bring the nose around and head for the grass to the side. The last thing that he thought about as the world went black was Maggie's face and laugh.

A month later Patrick got one of the pilots to drop him off at the Black Swan and he walked into the early evening quiet of the bar. He had just received his new orders on his return from the hospital. From Monday he would be moving into an intelligence role where his experience in combat could be put to use. He was making a good recovery, but the extensive injuries to his arm meant the end of his flying career; now he would be ensuring that he kept others safe in the skies. In one way he felt that he was abandoning those that he regarded

What's in a Name?

as family in their close knit squadron, but he also knew that it offered him the opportunity to fulfil a dream that was equally important.

Maggie was polishing glasses and looked up to greet the new customer with her usual smile but instead she took a deep breath. As he moved closer Patrick could see that there were tears in her glorious green eyes. Maggie stepped out from behind the bar and walked towards him, glancing at his arm in its sling and the scar that was etched into his forehead. She stood in front of him and neither spoke for a moment until he reached out his good arm to take her hand.

'Is there any chance that you might let me take you to the dance tomorrow night?'

She smiled through her tears. 'How are you going to be able to dance with only one free arm?'

He pulled her into him and looked down at the lips that he had imagined kissing so many times in the last few months.

'Don't worry Red… I'll manage just fine.'

QUEENIE

Queenie Denton contemplated the crumbs on the plate in front of her. She barely remembered eating the toast and marmalade and wondered if she was losing her marbles.

It was six weeks since her husband of fifty-five years, Donald, had died peacefully clasping the silver cross he had bought at a charity shop in the high street the month before. He was not a religious man, but he had worked for an insurance company as man and boy, and she supposed he thought it prudent at eighty years old to cover his bets. She on the other hand went to church every Sunday and was a member of the church ladies group that arranged the flowers and kept the place spotless between services.

They called themselves the Holy Dusters, and she realised with a pang that she missed seeing her friends every few days. They had been marvellous of course, bringing around Victoria sponges and sitting with her in the first few weeks, but she had then begun to ignore the doorbell; sitting in solitude in Donald's recliner.

She must make the effort and get back to normal. She could just imagine what her husband would have to say about the state of the house, and the fact that she had not put her make-up on for weeks.

There were a few other things she had neglected since Donald had suddenly collapsed and been rushed into hospital. She had cancelled her regular Wednesday morning hair appointment and she could see that her normally pristine and beautifully manicured nails needed immediate attention.

She picked up her plate, cup and saucer and popped them into the kitchen sink before reaching for the telephone on the wall.

Two days later, looking and feeling more like herself; Queenie put the telephone down from talking to Mavis who was in charge of the dusting rota. She would be starting back next Tuesday; giving her time to get her own house in order. But, with Donald gone and nobody to fuss over, she needed a project and immediately her mind veered to thoughts of her as yet single granddaughter Penny. Now there was a challenge if ever there was one.

Penny was a brilliant psychiatrist who worked at the local hospital. Tall and rather striking, she had never married, and at thirty-five didn't seem to have any interest in doing so. Queenie loved her dearly, but having set her heart on being a great grandmother before she followed Donald into the great beyond, she felt it was time for an intervention.

The following Saturday with her house back to spick and span order, Queenie piled a tray with cups, coffee pot and red velvet cupcakes and carried it into the living room where Penny was removing her coat and scarf.

'Here we are darling,' Queenie smiled warmly at her granddaughter, who came over and took the heavy tray from her.

'Those cupcakes look delicious Nana. Are you back to baking again?' Penny placed the tray on the coffee table and sat in the chair next to her grandmother.

'No dear, I must be honest, I bought them from the new bakery next to my hairdressers and I must admit to trying one or two already.'

What's in a Name?

Niceties out of the way, Queenie decided to get a few details ironed out before she outlined her project for her granddaughter.

'Penny,' she started hesitantly. 'I hope you don't mind me being a little indelicate, but are you in the wardrobe?'

Penny cocked her head to one side and contemplated her grandmother, barely able to contain her laughter.

'Whatever do you mean Nana,' she composed herself.

'Well, I was in the hairdressers the other day, reading a magazine where a young woman about your age said that she had recently come out of the wardrobe to her parents, and they had not been very understanding.'

'Ah… I get it now Nana; actually it is usually referred to as being in the closet, and do you know why she might have been in the closet?'

'Of course darling, I am not that old fashioned, and in fact when I was a young woman it was quite common for two maiden ladies to move in together and not to marry. It was understood that there was an arrangement and nobody really thought anything about it. Of course it was much more difficult when two young men moved in together; which never seemed fair to me.'

Penny was relieved to hear that her grandmother understood the situation so well, but felt that she ought to put her grandmother straight on her own state of affairs.

'Nana I'm not gay and I wondered why you should think that?' She looked at Queenie in amusement.

'Well, you have often said that you have no intention of marrying or having children, and I just feel that it is such a shame to go through life alone.' Queenie paused for a moment and gathered her thoughts.

'Marriage is not always perfect, and goodness knows I drove your poor grandfather to distraction with my little foibles. Not to say that he didn't have his own, although it was difficult to get him to admit it. But, our love was strong enough to weather any storm and I just wish that you could experience that for yourself.'

Penny looked down at her ringless hands and tried to forget that she was a psychiatrist for a moment, and just a granddaughter who was about to share her very private thoughts for the first time.

'Nana,' she began quietly. 'When I was at university I fell in love with another student. He was two years ahead of me studying medicine. We met at one of the dances and we clicked immediately.'

Queenie leant forward in her chair watching her normally composed granddaughter struggle to tell this story.

'Go on darling,' she encouraged smiling across the space between them.

'His name was Aaron Bernstein and came from Israel. We moved in to a flat together a year before he finished his degree, and he was planning on doing his hospital rotations here in England until I finished my own. However his parents came over to visit shortly before he graduated, and told him in no uncertain terms, that they would disown him if he chose to marry someone not of their faith.'

Tears rolled down Penny's cheeks and she took a tissue out of her handbag.

Queenie was speechless, she had not heard this story before and she was angry that her son, Penny's father, had kept it from her.

'Did your parents know about this Penny?' She tried not to sound hurt and angry.

'No, Nana, I told no-one, especially when Aaron felt that he could not go against his parents and disappoint them. He returned to Israel straight after graduation and I haven't

What's in a Name?

heard from him since.' She paused and looked at her grandmother's expression of dismay.

'I did try to find him by searching online for a number of years but I eventually gave up and tried to put him out of my mind.'

This was a bombshell indeed and Queenie felt herself getting very angry at this dreadful slight against her only granddaughter.

'I'm so sorry darling,' she reached across and held Penny's hand. 'Haven't you been out with anyone else in the last ten years that you might have had feelings for?'

Penny smiled at her grandmother's concerned face. 'I have dated quite a bit Nana, but never met anyone like Aaron. He was simply my soul mate and I don't want to settle for less.'

This disturbing conversation replayed over and over in Queenie's mind in the next few days and after her next visit to the hairdressers, and after reading a very interesting article, she contacted her friend Doris.

The next day she arrived at her friend's house looking immaculate in her a new emerald green jacket and her pearls. She was not going to make her debut on the international worldwide webby thing looking anything but her best.

Doris led her into her dining room where the two of them sat side by side in front of a computer screen.

'Now Queenie, you said that you wanted to find your granddaughter a soul mate online so I have got the links for some recommended dating sites we can try.' She looked over to her friend to see if they were on the same page.

'Actually Doris, I have something else in mind after reading an article in a magazine yesterday.

She slipped a piece of paper across the table to Doris who picked it up to study.

'Okay, that is an interesting approach,' and with that she typed in the link onto the screen.

Two weeks later Penny was surprised to get a phone call from her grandmother at nearly midnight, and was immediately concerned that Queenie was unwell.

She assured her granddaughter that all was fine, but she needed to see her on Saturday morning urgently. Queenie uttered a quick 'love you' and put the phone down.

Penny duly arrived at ten in the morning and was relieved to see that Queenie was resplendent in pink jacket and beautifully presented as normal. Her only concern was that she looked slightly flushed and over excited, and she wanted to get to the bottom of it right away.

'Okay Nana, I'm here so what is so urgent?'

Queenie placed her hand on her heart and took a deep breath.

'Darling, I know that you feel that there could never be another soul mate for you and I do understand that,' she paused before continuing in a rush 'I hope you don't mind but I have done something rather serious.'

'What have you done Nana?' Penny was not sure where this was leading but she had a suspicion that she was not going to enjoy it.

'Well darling, you said that it was several years since you last checked online to find Aaron, so I thought that I would give it a shot, and Doris and I have been investigating. Penny who had no idea that her grandmother even knew how to switch on a computer was stunned at this surprising development.

Seeing the bemused look on Penny's face, Queenie took her by the hand and led her into the living room where she pulled her down to sit beside her on the sofa.

'Darling, I found him, I found your Aaron.' Penny put a trembling hand over her mouth and stared at Queenie completely speechless.'

Queenie excitedly continued. 'I found him on this place called LinkedIn and it has to be the right one. He served in the Israeli army for ten years before going to America where he is a top heart surgeon at a large hospital in New York.'

'Oh my God Nana, I don't believe it.' Penny stared at her grandmother as if she had never seen her before.

'And that's not all,' Queenie continued. 'Doris is on LinkedIn too because of the fancy job that she had so she was able to send him a message thingy, asking him if he was the one who trained in England and knew a girl called Penny.'

Completely mortified Penny stood up and walked to the window. Her heart was thumping madly in her chest and she could barely breathe. She couldn't bring herself to believe that this would lead anywhere; after all he was probably married with children by now.

At that moment she saw a black taxi pull up outside the house and the back door open. A tall man with slightly greying hair got out and leant through the front window as he paid the driver. He turned and opened the gate, walking briskly to the front door. He turned as he caught a movement in the bay window and after a moment of simply staring at each other, he smiled, his eyes crinkling in a very familiar way.

She heard Queenie walking down the hall to open the door and then footsteps across the parquet flooring.

Penny held her breath with her eyes closed as she felt his presence behind her and then his two hands gently resting on her shoulders.

He pulled her back in to him and whispered in her ear.

'I am sorry I was not brave enough then. Please forgive me and tell me it is not too late.'

They did not hear the front door close or see Queenie as she walked down the path and disappeared from view.

She was smiling as she made her way to Doris's house; eager to get cracking on their next adventure online which was to sign up for one of those Mediterranean cruises in the Spring. She was sure Donald would not approve, but as Doris reminded her, you are only young once.

ROSEMARY

Rosemary viewed her face in the mirror. She sighed as she observed the crow's feet at the corner of her eyes. They said it was a sign of character and a sunny personality; crease lines from a life of laughter. That could be said to be true of most of the last twenty-five years of marriage to Malcolm. Rarely did a day go by that he had not teased her into a smile or offered up a pun that made her laugh despite the corniness.

It was not just the laughter that they had shared, but passions for theatre, the cinema, books and exotic foods. There was so little that they disagreed about over the years. Rosemary struggled to remember any real arguments that had intruded into the happiness that wrapped around them like a comforting blanket.

They had travelled far and wide across all the continents taking advantage of his generous salary and the occasional business trips that she accompanied him on. The scents and sights of Africa and India had thrilled them as they held hands and watched glorious sunsets. The rugged terrain of Alaska and the Rockies had tested their stamina and the deep blue colour of the Pacific Ocean had beguiled them. A storehouse of experiences all accompanied by love and laughter and a sense that it would last forever. They had never had children unfortunately, but Malcolm claimed to be happy to just have her all to himself.

But suddenly all that love and laughter was gone and the years together faded into wisps of elusive memory as each

What's in a Name?

day passed. Those friends that she had confided in about her grief and emptiness had offered advice and support for the last six months. They all assured her that was time to face the future head on. She needed to accept that she could not wallow in this self-pity and denial any longer.

She had laughed to herself when she first saw the website that Molly had pointed out to her one morning as they shared coffee in the village just after Christmas. An online dating agency that proudly boasted a near perfect record of finding your soul mate; that one person meant just for you. Molly had been on the site for nearly a year and she had certainly pushed the boundaries of those claims to the limit; she had kept their small circle of mutual friends very entertained with her experiences.

She had brought up the site on her laptop and Rosemary had sat beside her, browsing the various enticements offered by the men posting. Her eye had been immediately drawn to one post that Molly had marked. She read the words to herself, and then again aloud to fully understand what she was seeing. She had believed for so long that Malcolm was the one and only perfect match for her that she was shocked and intrigued at the same time.

Single, tall, fun loving and handsome 55 years old seeks long term relationship with attractive female 30–45 years old. Must have a good sense of humour, enjoy the theatre, cinema, fine dining and travelling to exotic locations. Located in London but willing to travel to meet.
Box Number 1596

She had looked over at Molly to share her amazement and found her staring down at her hands cupped around the coffee cup.

What's in a Name?

'Is something the matter Molly?' Rosemary was unused to Molly being subdued and quiet.

Slowly Molly looked up from her cappuccino and smiled fondly at her friend.

'I was going to meet this guy for dinner but changed my mind when I saw him sitting at the table in the restaurant," she paused and looked through the cafe window as if trying to choose her words carefully. "I know how much you still love Malcolm, but I think that it is time that you faced the reality of your situation and look to the future.'

Molly tapped the advertisement on the screen with her immaculately manicured nail. 'You need to arrange to meet this man and confront your fear of losing everything you have treasured from the past.'

The two women parted company outside the cafe and Rosemary drove home to the empty house that she had shared with Malcolm for so many years. It was far too big for the two of them especially when he was away on business trips alone leaving her for several weeks at a time. She had hoped at one point to fill the rooms with children's laughter, but somehow it was never the right time for one reason or another.

Rosemary knew that Molly was right. She could no longer hide away from life; she needed to face the future whatever it held. She rang her friend's mobile number and asked her to come over the next morning to help her upload a profile to the site to enable her to respond to the advertisement.

So here she was, getting ready for her first date in over twenty-five years with a man called Andrew. When her own profile had been activated, she had replied to the box number in his advertisement and over the next week they had exchanged a number of emails via the site. Although he was eager to know more about her, Rosemary had been reticent

What's in a Name?

to offer her personal email or too much information until she met him face to face.

She had changed her mind several times about what to wear for this first encounter, finally deciding to wear a new dress she had bought on a whim a few weeks ago. Malcolm had always insisted she looked perfect in pastel colours and this daring emerald green number would have certainly provoked some comment. She had also been to a new hairdresser this morning and requested a radical new look. Gone was the long brunette hair that Malcolm said suited her best; in its stead was a sleek blonde shoulder length bob.

Finally she stood in front of the long mirror in their bedroom and viewed the transformation. Rosemary took several moments to get used to the new image and then smiled as she decided that she liked it. Picking up a colourful floral scarf to put around her shoulders and grabbing her handbag, she walked down to the kitchen to order a taxi.

She deliberately arrived at the restaurant fifteen minutes early and was shown to a discreet table in the corner. Rosemary could not remember when she had been this nervous and sipped the water provided by the waiter when he left the two menus. She kept glancing at the door of the restaurant apprehensively. She knew that Andrew would have to ask directions to the table as he would not recognise her from the profile photo she had uploaded, particularly in the dimly lit room. On the table to the right of her place setting was a bulky envelope. Andrew in one of his recent emails had suggested that she might bring some photographs of the places that she had visited on her trips and that he would do likewise. A talking point to break the ice.

Closing her eyes she took a deep breath and tried to calm her nerves. When she opened them again she saw a tall, good looking man standing in the entrance to the dining area. He managed to get the attention of one of the waiters who then pointed out Rosemary sitting in the corner table. He walked confidently across with a warm smile on his face until he stood in front of her. Andrew looked into her eyes and he gasped.

'Hello Malcolm.' Rosemary attempted to keep the quiver out of her voice. 'I see that you are not at the New York head office after all this week. Please sit down as we have a great deal to talk about.'

Taken aback by his usually complacent wife's new look and the rigid set of her mouth, he complied ungraciously; flinging his coat on the back of one of the chairs. She pushed the envelope across the table towards him and as his fingers closed over the bulky package she smiled sadly.

'Perhaps we should start by discussing these divorce papers.'

SONIA

Sonia looked through the lead glass window of her bedroom, and watched as her three brothers disappeared into the distant forest. The dark trees swallowed them in an instant, and closing her eyes she imagined she was beside them; riding Anica her white filly. How she loved the trails through the dark woods that suddenly opened into sun dappled glades of wild flowers and mushrooms. But her father had banned her from accompanying her carefree brothers, decreeing that it was time at seventeen to adopt a more ladylike and regal demeanour.

Tears filled her eyes at the memory of her last discussion with her father this morning; standing before him in the cold and intimidating throne room.

'Sonia my child,' her father scratched his balding head. 'It is time to forget childish ways and prepare yourself for your marriage to Prince Aleksander on New Year's Eve.' Glaring at her from beneath his bushy eyebrows he continued, 'I will not listen to your complaining and disobedience any longer; is that understood?'

He contemplated his only daughter, and remembered his wife's wise words on how to deal with their wilful youngest child.

'You must remember that the security of our kingdom depends on an advantageous union with all of our neighbours. Your brothers are promised to princesses on three corners of our realm, and when you marry the heir to Pokova to the north, we will have peace and prosperity for the future.'

He sighed and steeled his heart as watched her crestfallen beautiful face. 'Your mother and I did not meet until our wedding day and we have had a most happy union, being also blessed with you and your brothers. We are royalty, and arranged marriages are as much part of our lives as your silk dresses and other privileges'.

Sonia bit her lip and silenced her response. She had been attempting to persuade her parents for the last two months that she could not marry a man that she had not met, and had not even seen a likeness of. Her shoulders slumped wearily and she curtsied to her father, asking permission to go to her rooms. The king waved her away in frustration and watched as the dispirited girl left the chamber.

Petar, Jakov and Henrik would be gone for several hours and she resigned herself to sitting in the window alcove and watching the palace staff going about their preparations for the grand feast tomorrow. The courtyard and kitchen gardens were bustling with activity. The cook and his assistants were unpacking tradesmen's carts and gathering vegetables to accompany roast venison and turkey. In the distance she could see the giant farm horses pulling the cart holding the majestic tree harvested from the dense forest and destined for the ballroom.

Prince Aleksander was due to arrive today, but protocol demanded that she wait until she was formally introduced to him at the ball. Her brothers had met him at the annual boar hunt in the summer, and she had pestered them to tell her more about him.

Unfortunately her three brothers loved to tease her and refused to talk about the prince at all; making faces at each other in merriment. A thought struck her and she gasped at the possible reason for their silence. He must be ugly, she thought, or perhaps stupid or had a nasty temper. Her nervousness only increased and she clasped her arms around her body in despair.

As she looked out of the window a flash of movement caught her eye. From the cobbled stable yard came a tall blonde man leading a jet black stallion. He was wearing a loose white shirt and leather jerkin, but it didn't conceal the fact that he was very muscular as well as handsome. Feeling a little flushed, Sonia wondered why she had not seen this groom before. She also wondered why she had not heard the normally observant chamber maids gossiping about the new addition to the staff.

She watched as the man and horse moved gracefully down to the paddock, and she opened the window so that she could see more clearly. The cold winter air rushed into the room but pulling her shawl closer about her shoulders, she settled down to watch the proceedings.

The man released the horse and moved to the centre of the round paddock. He flicked a fine whip onto the sawdust behind the horse, which responded by trotting around the outside of the ring… Another flick and the stallion turned and moved in the opposite direction. The elegance of both man and beast were magnificent; totally absorbing Sonia in the performance. After several minutes, the man dropped the whip to his side and turned to walk towards the gate… The horse stopped in his tracks and followed, gently nudging his shoulder to gain the groom's attention. At the gate the man pivoted and placed his right hand at the top of horse's forehead; leaning into him. They stood for several minutes; man and beast as one.

Sonia caught her breath and stuck her head out of the window, better to capture this intense and beautiful moment. The groom turned away from the horse and as he did so he looked up. He saw Sonia inelegantly hanging out of the

What's in a Name?

window and smiled; even from this distance it was devastatingly effective. She ducked back inside and slammed the window shut. The impudence of the man, and to crown it all, this was just the sort of behaviour that her father had been so critical of.

That evening her mother knocked on her door and ushered through two maids with laden trays. She had also brought the palace seamstress who carried a linen wrapped garment over her arm. Sonia loved her beautiful mother and hoped that over their supper she might be able to win her over to her side.

She had heard her brothers arrive back an hour earlier, clattering into the courtyard and calling for Anton the head groom to come and collect their horses. As they had noisily run up the steps to the main entrance of the palace, Sonia had been tempted to peek out of the window to see if Anton had anyone assisting him. But she had dismissed this foolishness. Tomorrow she would be betrothed, and married on New Year's Eve. She must put all these romantic notions from her mind. However, part of her wished with all her might that she could be just a simple maid, who could dream of love and marriage with that devastatingly attractive but unobtainable man.

Her mother eventually left Sonia's chambers having remained resolute on the upcoming marriage. But she had smiled at her daughter's determined efforts, whilst reminding her that she had a royal duty to obey her father. Hanging on the front of the door to Sonia's dressing room was a very beautiful pale blue dress. The ball gown was edged with matching satin and violet flowers draped across one shoulder down to the slender waist. However, even this sensational garment did little to lift her mood as she contemplated how tomorrow would change her life forever.

What's in a Name?

Early the next evening the guests for the Christmas ball began to arrive in their carriages. Whilst waiting to dress, Sonia kept watch from the window hoping to catch sight of the groom as the horses were led away. Her maid assisted her into her ball gown, and gently tucked in an odd strand of jet black hair which had drifted from the elaborate upswept style. Sonia stood in front of her full length mirror and despite appreciating that she looked every inch a princess, she felt coldness deep in her heart. She had to face the fact that she would never know the kind of love that other girls were privileged to receive. Her father had won, and very soon she would be leaving the palace and going to a strange land, far away from those who had loved and protected her until this moment.

Sonia carefully descended the red carpet of the curved staircase, eyeing the clusters of guests in an attempt to identify the man she was going to be spending the rest of her life with. Most were known to her, and as she moved between them they smiled and bowed. She saw that her father was at the end of the throne room with her mother, three brothers and a tall stranger with his back to the room.

Her father looked up and saw her, beckoning her over and touching the stranger on his shoulder. As Sonia reached the group, the elegantly dressed man turned and she looked into startling blue eyes. She gasped as she recognised the shaggy blonde hair and the broad shoulders, blushing to the roots of her hair.

'Your Highness, may I introduce my daughter, Princess Sonia.'

Her father took her right hand and placed it into the large palm of the man in front of her.

'Sonia meet your betrothed, Prince Aleksander of Pokova.'

Breathlessly Sonia looked down at his broad and suntanned hand.

A deep voice broke into her scattered thoughts. 'I believe we have glimpsed each other before Princess.'

She looked up into his smiling face and her lips trembled as she fumbled for a response.

Sensing her discomfort, Prince Aleksander continued, ' I was working with Kyros this afternoon when you noticed us. He is my betrothal present to you and I hope you will ride him back to Pokova with me after our wedding.'

Sonia's beaming smile and gentle squeeze of his hand gave him his answer, and as he led her off to the dance floor for their first waltz, she heard her father behind her.

'Somebody get me a brandy… A very large brandy'.

THERESA

'Come on let's whip into that lane over there.'
'No, I am fine here, look the line is moving already.'
'Are you kidding me?' He glared at her in frustration. 'We are going to be here till Christmas at this rate and the game starts in twenty minutes.'

She shrugged her shoulders. 'It's only football for goodness sake, just be patient.'

'Patient, patient!' Hands in pockets he made a face.

'I came shopping with you didn't I? He put a hand on her shoulder.

'Come on Theresa, please we only have three items and that line is much shorter.'

She shrugged his hand off and took a deep breath.
'She doesn't like me.'
'Who doesn't like you?'
'The woman in that checkout.'

'Excuse me!' He looked at her in disbelief. 'What are you talking about?'

'I have been through that checkout several times when I was in a hurry and each time she has made rude comments.'

'Love, you're losing it babe, big time.' She glared at him.

'Okay last time I went through that checkout with a pizza and ice-cream; she said that she could see why I was fat.'

'You must have imagined it doll.' Laughingly he grabbed her waist fondly. 'I love every inch of you and you are not fat just cuddly.'

152

What's in a Name?

'Alright, I'll prove it to you.' She turned and stomped off to the now empty check-out and waved the first item, which happened to be a packet of fish fingers, under the scanner.

A slightly metallic female voice spat out of the speaker. 'Oh my, still picking the fat options I see.'

Theresa turned to her husband and gave him a glare.... 'Well, do you believe me now?'

'It must be a wind up... Candid Camera or one of those stupid programmes. Put another item through.'

Theresa put the two other items under the scanner one by one. The voice smugly pronounced. 'That will be four pounds and eleven pence and half a stone madam.'

Fuming Theresa put her debit card into the reader and completed the transaction. She threw the offending items into her bag for life.

'Okay Theresa let me have a go.' Her husband picked up some gum from the stand next to the checkout and passed it under the scanner.

'Hello handsome,' spoke a silky sexy voice. 'What are you doing for the rest of my life?'

USHER

Usher Matthews was a good looking man. Tall, with jet black hair inherited from his Italian grandfather, he could charm the birds out of the trees… or out of a nightclub and into the back of his car which was as flash as he was. The life and soul of any party, he would splash the cash and whilst the fairer sex adored him, males clustered around him on the off chance some of his luck with the girls might rub off.

He had fallen into the estate agency business through sheer luck when he left school. His best friend's father owned several offices in the surrounding county and he offered Usher the opportunity to join the firm along with his son as a trainee. His friend soon discovered that he was unable to come out from under his friend's shadow, leaving to join the army, but Usher was born for the job. He worked his way up to branch manager in an exclusive area by his mid-twenties, and as a salesman he excelled. Sometimes his unsuspecting clients would wonder why they ended up with the house they did. Good old Usher always popped round and reinforced all the positives about the property they might have overlooked even when the back wall of the house subsided.

Usher rarely took any of his expanding group of acquaintances home to the modest terrace house where he was brought up. To be honest, his parents, who were quite shy and retiring, had no idea how they had produced this charismatic son of theirs. His father privately wondered if he had not been switched at birth; especially on the rare occasion he joined

What's in a Name?

Usher down the pub for a pint. He would sit there quietly sipping his beer and watch as people gathered to bask in the radiance that emanated from his offspring.

More and more he refused his son's infrequent invitations. Eventually he and his equally mystified wife sold their home and moved to Bognor to retire. Usher barely noticed their departure and would phone once in a while and threaten to come down for a weekend. His parents soon realised that these promises were empty, resigning themselves to the fact that their son was far too involved in his own life to be bothered about them.

Whilst apparently an open book as far as the world was concerned, there were a couple of things that Usher liked to conceal from people. One was his pathological fear of snakes that did not enhance his macho and gym-toned public persona. At five years old his well-meaning parents had bought him a Jack-in-the box type toy for his birthday. He had screamed like a girl when a two foot and very life-like banded snake had launched itself at him from the stupid thing.

The other secret was his little gambling habit. He did love those horses but unfortunately they did not love him. This had not been too bad when property was selling like hotcakes, but with the downturn, his commission was as extinct as a Dodo. This little matter was resolved by the charm offensive, seduction and marriage to Rebecca, the daughter of a multi-millionaire retailer who gave them a rather nice cash settlement on their wedding day. Just in time, as recently the account with his bookie had plummeted deeply into the red. Their frequent telephone conversations had become downright hostile.

Apart from the gambling there were also some other side activities that Usher kept from his wife who would look at him adoringly when he walked through the door each evening.

What's in a Name?

She seemed to accept that he needed to work late a couple of evenings a week, taking potential clients to dinner or showing properties in the longer summer evenings. He was careful to make sure that he didn't bring home evidence of his dalliances, thinking himself rather clever at having his cake and eating it.

His wife was pretty enough he supposed, but he also thought she was not very bright. He did however appreciate the generous monthly allowance that her father paid into his daughter's bank account which he offered to manage for her. She had agreed readily enough, and to his knowledge never bothered to check her bank balance. Usher decided to do a little mining into the account and gradually syphoned off thousands of pounds to cover his debts over the next few months. To celebrate he suggested that he and Rebecca head off to Thailand for a second honeymoon.

They stayed at the best hotel close to the sandy white beach where the calm waters invited the visitors in for swimming and water sports. For the more adventurous, deep sea snorkeling was on offer, and surprisingly the normally reserved Rebecca, took to the activity like a duck to water. She headed off with one of the undersea guides every day for several hours returning exhausted and full praise for her guide's patient tutelage.

Usher was a little miffed if he was honest at not being the centre of attention. He got a bit bored lying by the pool and sipping a selection of exotic drinks off the cocktail menu. He spent some time flirting with some of the younger bikini clad sun worshippers; knowing that he would be unlikely to get away with anything more in these restricted confines.

At the start of the second week Rebecca suggested that he might come with her out to a small reef just a five minute swim off shore. Taken by surprise by her rather seductive smile and the sight of her now bronzed body in her bikini he nodded his agreement. He donned his mask and after some tips from Rebecca on how to breathe and dive with his apparatus, they headed away from the beach.

He had to admit it was pretty stunning seeing all the brightly coloured fish and coral life and he relaxed into the adventure. Suddenly, his wife appeared right in front of him with her hand behind her back. She gestured to him to rise to the surface.

They both removed their masks and as the warm water lapped around his neck he saw Rebecca's gloved hand reach out towards him rapidly. He felt an excruciating pain in his neck and looked down to see the brightly coloured, writhing body of a snake. As his vision blurred he screamed like a girl and stared at his wife treading water calmly.

As his eyes met Rebecca's cold and steady gaze, she mouthed just one word.

'Surprise.'

VANESSA

Vanessa cradled the cooling mug of tea between her hands and debated getting up and putting the central heating on early. It was just after six o'clock, and having had a sleepless night, she was feeling colder than this spring morning warranted.

She was waiting for the national bulletin to finish and the local report to come on. The images from the top news story last night were still playing in her mind; as they had done as she tried to fall asleep in the early hours. She usually lay awake waiting for her son Jack to get home, but even when she heard him open the front door and creep up the stairs, she had failed to find comfort in his safe return.

The local news report began and she turned up the volume on the remote just a fraction, as she didn't want to wake Jack yet. The announcer repeated the basic facts about the assault and murder of a fifteen year old girl; now named as Tracy Martin two nights ago. A photograph of a young beautiful girl with long blonde hair, smiling happily into the camera, flashed up on screen.

They also replayed the CCTV footage from last night of the victim in the company of a group of young people, walking through the precinct two hours before her body had been found.

This was followed by additional footage they had just received; captured an hour afterwards, showing Tracy walking arm in arm with a young male. The couple had disappeared into an alley behind a restaurant. The camera had picked

What's in a Name?

up the man leaving twenty minutes later but no sign of his companion. It was impossible to see his features as his grey hoodie was pulled up over his head, but as the cameras tracked his progress along the main street, it was clear that he had a slight limp as he favoured his left leg.

As a mother she could only imagine how this young girl's devastated parents must be feeling this morning. Since Jack's father died ten years ago she had felt the weight of being a single parent, and the responsibility of being both mother and father. He was an only child, and she had tried to make sure that he was not spoilt, and that he understood the value of the important things in life, such as hard work, kindness and responsibility.

She felt she had done a pretty good job, and the thought of losing him was unthinkable. She played back in her mind the events of the last year, and how she had felt Jack pulling away from her. At first she had accepted that it was normal for a young man to want to distance himself from his mum, and make a life for himself with friends. But now, as she contemplated the devastating loss that this young girl's family were facing, she knew that she had to take action.

As the report finished, with a request from the police for any witnesses to come forward with information to a dedicated incident telephone number, Vanessa put down her now cold tea, heading into the hall and up the stairs.

She pushed open the door as quietly as possible to her son's bedroom. She could hear his steady breathing as she crossed over to stand by his bedside. At nearly twenty he still retained his boyish face, and with his blonde hair across his forehead and long eyelashes, he looked young and vulnerable. The sweet natured boy she loved so much. She sat on the chair against the wall and watched her son as he slept; seemingly oblivious to the world and its potential evil.

What's in a Name?

How many nights had the parents of Tracy Martin sat and watched their daughter sleep in an attempt to keep her safe from that same evil? She wiped the tears from her cheeks as she imagined their sorrow and anger at what had happened to their child.

Slowly she stood and crossed to the laundry basket filled to the brim with her son's washing. She picked up his discarded sweatshirt thrown casually on the top of the other clothes and held it close to her chest inhaling his familiar scent. She replaced it on top of the basket and carried it carefully through the door; pulling it closed behind her. Satisfied that she had not woken her son, Vanessa headed downstairs, placing the washing in the hall next to Jack's sneakers, which he had kicked off before creeping upstairs.

It was now nearly seven, and it would not be long before the houses in the street would be filled with light, as families prepared breakfast before heading out to school and to jobs. She went into the kitchen and pulled the door shut behind her; reaching for her mobile phone on the counter. She dialled the number that she had written down an hour ago, and waited for an answer at the other end.

She clung to the phone desperately and tried to find the courage that she knew she would need for the outcome of this conversation. She had been gifted this night with her son, and that was something that Tracy's parents had not been given.

She relived the moment when she had recognised her son in the grainy video they had broadcast last night, as he had walked at the edge of the group in the precinct. She had intended to ask him about it when he woke up this morning, and to break the news to him that one of his young friends was dead.

But that was before she saw the second video of Tracy and her companion this morning, entering the alley, and then the

What's in a Name?

footage of the man leaving alone and limping along the street. A limp caused by a broken leg from falling out of a tree seven years ago. An indistinct figure of a man that only a mother would recognise.

In the dark Jack had clearly not realised that his grey hoodie had several strands of long blonde hair attached to it when he threw it in the laundry basket that night, nor that his sneakers by the front door, had what looked like drops of blood across the laces.

With tears rolling down her cheeks, she realised that a man was talking to her at the other end of the line.

'Hello, is anyone there?'

'Yes, I have some information about the attack on Tracy Martin two nights ago.

WALTER

Somebody mentioned that they had heard that his name was Walter. He was a funny old duck who said little, giving you a discouraging look if you passed the time of day, or suggested sitting with him in the pub. He would nurse his pint of beer, the only one he would have for the two hours he visited The Crown each Friday, and he spent that time staring at the door as if waiting for someone he knew.

With his scruffy appearance and lack of hygiene it was difficult to determine Walter's age. Some said he was in his 80s but others thought he might be even older than that. He didn't bother anyone, although the landlord would have liked a little more custom from him over the two hours. However it would not be good for business to be seen ejecting a frail old man; despite his musty odour. That was until he ambled in one day with his stick in one hand and a filthy mongrel on a lead in the other.

Bill, who had run The Crown for twenty years, didn't have a problem with dogs coming into the public bar, but this one felt the need to cock his leg against the first table leg he came across, marking his territory. Diplomacy was required, and being the summer months, Bill suggested that Walter and his new companion take their business outside to the beer garden, where there was a very nice table facing the back door to the pub.

Walter gave Bill one of his looks and led the scruffy mongrel outside and parked himself; indicating that he required his usual pint to be brought to him. Resigned, but happy that this matter had been resolved peacefully, Bill brought out the beer and commented that it was on the house. He received a curt nod in return and shaking his head in exasperation he returned to the bar where his staff were mopping up the offending yellow puddle with some bleach.

Bill was a good man and he made enquiries of other locals as to where Walter lived, and if they knew of his circumstances. It was thought that he rented a small terrace house two streets over, and some commented that they had seen him in the corner shop and post office from time to time, collecting his pension and buying a few staples such as bread and jam.

Thankfully the weather was dry for the next few weeks and Walter and his new friend would now enter the beer garden from the side; sitting at their table waiting for the requisite pint to be delivered. The old man would carefully count out some silver and copper coins to the exact amount of the pint to indicate that he was intent on not accepting it free.

Bill noticed a slight difference in Walter's appearance, and in fact the dog looked a little more nourished and cleaner than during his first visits. He wondered who was having a good influence over whom in this partnership; suspecting the dog was responsible. The pub had a thriving food business and there were always scraps left after lunch. Bill began taking out a bowl of these bits of meat and vegetables; putting them down under the table much to the delight of the dog who dived right in. Walter said nothing but he did offer a brief nod before Bill returned inside to the bar.

The weather began to turn into autumn and Bill knew that it was going to start getting too cold for the old man to sit outside. And sure enough the following Friday Walter walked into the bar with his dog and sat down at his usual table. This time the dog behaved itself and lay down by his owner's feet.

What's in a Name?

By now there had been a marked improvement in the scruffiness of both man and beast and Bill resigned himself to their presence in the bar. He smiled to himself as he pulled the pint of beer, thinking that the old boy was to be admired for his tenacity and spirit.

Regulars to the bar began stopping to talk to the dog who responded politely whilst leaning back against Walter's legs. Soon patrons were slipping the odd piece of steak or chicken to the animal who took the offered titbit daintily, licking the proffered fingers. Although Walter had tidied himself up considerably, he still looked too scrawny, and Bill came up with a plan. As Walter was getting up to leave he handed him a carrier bag with some cartons inside.

'Something for the old dog over the weekend Walter,' he smiled at the stony face in front of him. 'Just some leftovers from lunch that will only go to waste.'

With a quick nod, Walter took the bag and with the dog eagerly nosing the plastic, they walked out the door and into the wintery weather.

On the following Friday, Bill's mother, a spritely 85 year old arrived for her annual two weekly visit. Ethel had left the town some twenty years ago to live with her sister in Margate, but she loved coming back to the pub she and her husband had run for 40 years, taking it over from her parents when they retired. The place held happy memories and apart from Bill, she had brought up four other children in the small flat above the bar. They were all dispersed around the country, but they would all take the opportunity to visit whilst she was here to have a family party.

Ethel had been born in the main bedroom upstairs along with a twin brother. He had not wanted to stay in the town or follow his father into the family business. He had chosen to leave instead. Joining the army in 1952 and being deployed

What's in a Name?

to Korea shortly afterwards. As she sat on the edge of the bed in that same bedroom, she ran her fingers over the black and white photograph of the two of them sitting at a table in the back garden. Her brother Donald had a pint in front of him and his arms around her shoulders. They were laughing and playing around for the camera, a gift to their father for his birthday. That was the last time she had seen Donald. They had a few letters during the next year but they revealed little but basic daily life in the army. After the war ended in 1953 they waited to hear about his next leave but nothing arrived.

Eventually Ethel's father contacted his regiment only to discover that Donald had received a medical discharge three months before and that they had no forwarding address.

The family had searched for him everywhere and even got a private detective involved. Eventually, after two years, they found out that he had immigrated to Australia where all efforts to find him proved futile. It broke their hearts and they spent the rest of their lives wondering what had happened to him.

Ethel sighed as she remembered those tough days. Of course so much more was known about PTSD these days, and the doctors she had spoken to felt that was probably the reason for him shunning his family. Sorrowfully she placed the photograph back on the dresser and prepared to go and greet some of the old regulars who were coming in to join her in a drink.

Sure enough, when she arrived in the bar, there was a warm welcome from her old friends. Bill looked on smiling as he saw his mother embracing the people she had grown up with and served for all those years. The door opened and in walked Walter and his dog, clearly unsettled by the crowd of people gathered in their path and the noisy celebrations going on. He looked like he was about to turn around and

What's in a Name?

leave, but Bill knew that both he and the dog would probably go hungry over the weekend without their normal leftovers. He stepped out from behind the bar and circled around the group greeting his mother; clearing the path to Walter's usual table. Hesitantly the man and dog navigated their way across the room and sat down warily; the dog leaning protectively against Walter's leg.

At that moment the crowd parted and Bill saw his mother smiling across at the three of them. Then she grabbed the arm of one of the people next to her and looked as if she was about to faint. Bill rushed across and grabbed a bar stool for her to sit on.

'Mum, whatever's the matter, don't you feel well?' He put his arm around Ethel's shoulders, but she pushed him gently away and pointed across the bar.

'That's Walter and his dog Mum, you don't know him. He has only been coming in for the last few months.' He followed Ethel's gaze and was amazed to see Walter on his feet, tears pouring down his face into his newly trimmed beard.

As the crowd of people moved back, the old man with his dog at his side, walked slowly across the carpet to stand before Bill and his mother.

'I came to see you but you had gone and I thought you were dead.' The regulars looked at each other in astonishment at the first complete sentence they had heard from Walter.

Ethel moved away from the protective arms of her son, and reaching out a trembling hand, she gently touched the front of Walter's wrinkled jacket.

'Oh Donald, you have come home love, you have come home.'

XENIA

Your name is Xenia, after your Greek grandmother, whose wrinkled complexion smelt of roses and almond oil. I remember the hot summers of our visits as we played on the rocks beneath her stone house; working up an appetite for the platters of goat's cheese, olives and warm bread. The loaves were taken straight from the wood stove; handled carefully with well-worn hessian rags, and served up on the rough wooden table in her wild garden. I remember being fascinated by her hands as they sliced thick warm chunks with an ancient serrated bread knife. They were blackened from nearly 80 years in the sun, with dark-rimmed nails from digging into the soil for home grown vegetables.

She was still a beautiful woman, who loved to have her long black and grey hair gently brushed in the twilight; sipping delicately from her glass of rose pink wine. Happy sighs filled the scented air; encouraging continued effort. We dreaded her tears as we left to catch the ferry at the end of summer, with her whispered goodbyes and pleas for us to return again the next year, remaining in our minds for weeks afterwards.

But one summer only my father made the journey, to stay just a week to bury his beloved mother, with her silver backed hair brush and a small bottle of almond oil resting in her hands.

That was ten years ago and I have been saving up her name to give to you, my first child. From the moment I knew that I was carrying you in my womb, I felt certain that you would be a girl and worthy of this much loved name. As the

What's in a Name?

months passed, and I felt that first movement beneath my hand, I began to talk to you of your name and the woman who owned it with such grace. Sometimes when I listened to music playing softly in the background, I would feel a flutter, as if you were dancing in time to the tune. I would imagine Xenia, swaying and clapping her hands in delight, lost in the gentle songs that my father played on his guitar after our evening meal. I knew she would be so happy that I had named you after her.

My time with my grandmother was too short, but I had saved up the stories to tell you, as well as photographs we took during those summers. I would tell you those tales as we rocked, still joined together, in the chair in the newly painted nursery. I promised to show you the embarrassing snaps of your mother when a girl, dressed in her bathing suit with face filled with sticky baklava. I imagined taking you back to Greece to see where you came from, and to visit Xenia's grave to lay some blossom, and to show her how beautiful you are. I was certain that your hair would be raven black and that you would love almonds.

Your father laughed at me as I waddled around the house in search of more feta cheese and pickled onions. He said that there must be two of you, or that you were really a big bouncing boy; destined to be a rugby player. He would lay his head on my stomach and listen to your heartbeat; loving it when you kicked against his hand. We had chosen not to know the gender of our baby. I already knew it was a girl to be called Xenia, and your father just wanted a baby who was healthy that we would love.

I knew the moment you had gone. All was still where you had been so active. I thought you must be sleeping, and lay in the hospital bed resting, waiting for that kick and ripple, telling me you wanted my attention. But the cold gel, and pressure of the machine in a doctor's hand, broke the spell. Your father and I held each other as we cried at our loss.

The love I feel for you will not diminish or change throughout my life. It comforts me to imagine you holding the hand of your great-grandmother, as you twirl to the music of a guitar. I see you eating baklava with sticky fingers, and her washing your hands and face lovingly, with rose scented water. I know that you are safe now, and that one day, we will meet face to face, and I will recognise you as the child of my heart. One day the three of us will sit in that wild garden, and laugh in the sunshine.

My two beloved Xenias…

YVES

Yves Bertrand spoke English impeccably with a sexy French accent. When romancing a beautiful woman he used anything and everything in his arsenal. He was now in his late thirties, and had spent the last twenty years acquiring an encyclopedic knowledge of the trivia of the world. The vast majority of middle-aged women that he honoured with his attention were delighted at his acerbic wit and ability to name the world's most influential fashion designers. Not to mention his knowledge of the latest season's 'must have' shoes and handbags.

The majority of the women were divorcees or widows with time on their hands and money in their accounts. Their generosity had financed his activities and allowed him to buy a spectacular villa in the Greek islands. Along with a substantial amount tucked away in off shore accounts, Yves had sufficient to fund his early retirement; which he had decided would be at the age of forty.

With only a year to go before his income would be reliant on bank interest rates; Yves decided that this summer on the French Riviera would have to be exceptionally profitable. He consulted with the various concierges of the top hotels who were on his payroll. It was money well spent and within days, Yves received a coded text message to his burner phone, indicating that there was a big fish ready to be reeled in.

A lesser man would have felt guilty about the methods used to part vulnerable older women from their cash, but

Yves believed in giving value for money and his conquests seldom went away without happy memories. He had to admit however that it was becoming more difficult to play the role of amorous partner without some form of enhancement, and there were days when he wished he might retire sooner than the end of the season.

He received this particular text from the concierge at a luxuriously appointed hotel owned by a Saudi Prince, newly opened and a magnet for this season's divorcees. The penthouse suite had been rented for a month by a mysterious guest who would be occupying the opulent accommodations on her own. This was indeed promising and Yves selected his most recent acquisition from his wardrobe; congratulating himself on his foresight in buying the expensive but eye-catching dinner jacket. An hour later and dressed to kill, Yves walked casually into the hotel's garden restaurant and slipped the manager a suitably high valued bank note. He was whisked elegantly between the tables and the guests dipping into their caviar and duck breasts, and was seated at a table opposite a woman eating alone.

Surreptitiously, Yves peered over and around his menu at his target. She was stunning he had to admit. In her mid-forties perhaps; but possibly a little older. He would need to inspect her skin more closely to find the tell-tale signs of any cosmetic surgery. Long dark hair cascaded around her shoulders and her lightly tanned arms rested gently on the table in front of her. A waiter arrived and placed a covered plate in front of the attractive diner, and with a flourish, lifted the lid to reveal a whole lobster with a salad garnish. Delicately the woman picked up her fork and began to eat the white and succulent flesh. Yves found it very seductive and smiled to himself. Perhaps this summer was going to be more enjoyable than he had anticipated.

What's in a Name?

♪   At that moment the woman looked up from her lobster and stared right back at Yves with stunningly green eyes, penetrating deep into his soul. He fought against the wave of desire that swept through him with devastating effect. But he was already lost, and for the first time in his life, Yves Bertrand was in love with someone other than himself.

As a waiter hovered at his shoulder to take his order, the woman lifted her hand and beckoned Yves across to join her. He rose from his chair and arriving by her side, picked up the elegantly outstretched hand, kissing the jasmine scented skin at the base of the wrist. The woman smiled at him knowingly and he pulled out the chair beside her and sat down.

He barely remembered ordering the same dish as his new conquest. He was too busy thanking his lucky stars that this last summer was going to be the most delectable of his professional career.

Three weeks later as Yves and Christina lay side by side in the palatial king-sized bed in her suite, he reflected on his good fortune. He turned his head to watch her as she slept, exhausted by his amorous skills of last night. He smiled to himself and began formulating his new plan in his head. He had discovered that Christina was the 45 year old widow of a multi-billionaire who had collapsed suddenly at the age of seventy on the golf course. Although there had been three other wives and numerous children, he had left his newly acquired wife over fifty million along with a wonderful home in Monaco. She had been devastated to lose this wonderful man after only eighteen months of marriage and she had sobbed in Yves arms as she recounted her unspeakable loss on the second night of their acquaintance.

Yves in turn had admitted to owning a stunning villa in Greece. He still felt unwilling to admit to the magnitude of his bank holdings, but hinted at a generous income from a family trust fund. This had reassured Christina that she was in the company of a man of substance; unlike some of the admirers she had encountered in the last few months. She had relaxed into a sensual and delightful relationship that she hoped would last longer than the original month she had planned on staying.

Two days before her departure back to Monaco, Yves asked Christina a question that he had sworn would not pass his lips. Her acceptance, accompanied by tears and a substantial amount of kissing, elevated his emotions to previously unimagined heights. A hurried wedding was planned, and it was decided that Christina would sell her Monaco home and they would live in the villa in Greece, until such time as they could buy a more opulent property together.

Yves could not believe his good fortune. Not only had he found a beautiful companion for his retirement, but she was bringing with her a fortune that far outstripped his own few millions.

The sun shone as the two of them left the registry office with their witnesses trailing behind. Two passing tourists had been well paid for their services and had been only too happy to accept the invitation. The jubilant couple returned to the hotel and picked up Christina's several pieces of luggage. Within hours they were on their way to Greece and the love nest that waited for them.

Yves new wife suggested that it might be prudent for her to make a will to ensure that there be no challenge from her step-children should the unthinkable happen to her, and a local lawyer complied with her wishes. The document, leaving everything to Yves was signed and witnessed and placed in the safe of the villa. Yves at this point felt that he should of course reciprocate and detailed all his various bank accounts in his own will, leaving everything to his beautiful wife. She

What's in a Name?

was grateful for his consideration, and told him how happy she was that they were so fortunate to have found each other.

The next six months were spent in blissful indolence and even the thought of selling the villa and buying another was temporarily shelved. They loved their home's cool marble interior and the sloping garden that went down to the beach and sunlit sea. Their happiness was complete.

Then out of the blue tragedy struck. Yves was enjoying his morning swim a few hundred feet from the beach, when he felt a gripping pain in his chest and found himself unable to breathe. He lifted his hand to try and get the attention of Christina as she sat on the sand reading a book waiting for him to finish his swim. For a moment before he slipped beneath the waves, he thought he saw her smile and lift her hand to wave at him, but those images, like his last breath, were gone within seconds.

A year later when all the paperwork had been completed, Christina sat at the table on the terrace where she and Yves had enjoyed their breakfasts in the sunshine. In a metal waste bin sat a neat stack of shredded paper. Striking a match, Christina dropped it into the pile, watching it catch light. As she observed her old life go up in flames, she stroked the file of new documents in her name that gave her ownership of the villa, and the small fortune in the off shore bank accounts.

She had been down to her last 100,000 dollars when she had booked that hotel suite. But with her looks beginning to fade she knew this was probably the last summer of her professional career. There had been no husband, just a succession of much older men that she had nursed in the last years of their lives. Some had been more than generous in their wills to their devoted nurse; little knowing that their end had been hastened by rejuvenating potions. Over the years she would find new victims by spending the summer in one of the less expensive hotels along this stretch of the coast, but dining at the more luxurious accommodations. Like Yves she had paid the concierges well for their information. Most knew of Yves and his activities and suspected that he had earned substantially on the basis of their information. They also rather resented his success with the ladies and they were looking forward to him receiving some of his own medicine. And at the end of the day, a beautiful woman's money bought a little more loyalty than his.

However, Christina regretted that the handsome and attentive Yves had to pay the ultimate price for their love. But she could not afford for him to find out that her house in Monaco and her fifty million was fictitious. He had begun to suggest that they sell this villa and go to live in tax exile in Monaco. The final nail in his coffin was his announcement two days before he died, that he had booked flights leaving in a week so that they could check out properties.

She could remain in this beautiful villa now, living in luxury for the rest of her life. She would miss Yves but knew that there were plenty of young men who would find her mature beauty alluring and possibly lucrative. She might have retired from her professional life as a nurse and murderer, but there was plenty of scope for some innocent fun.

ZOE

Madame Zoe looked at the screen in front of her and watched the teenage girl in the waiting room. She was her next client and looked nervous; as many did who came to consult the renowned fortune teller, in her little oasis in the back streets of the town.

These few minutes observing her next client were important before meeting them for the first time. Were they nervous, excited, and worried? That gave her some clues as to what direction their consultation might go. Added to the extensive report that her assistant Marjorie had compiled, this allowed Madame Zoe to tailor her reading to each specific client's needs with outstanding results.

For example the young woman waiting for her fortune and fate to be revealed was called Sandra Johnson, and was twenty years old. She worked at a solicitor's office in the main street, and was currently in a relationship with a young mechanic called Steve. Unfortunately this union of three years was going through a tough patch, as Steve had been fooling around with Tracy; one of Sandra's closest friends.

Since her 18th birthday, the girl had been trying to find her birth mother. Unfortunately, it would appear that the official agency were finding it difficult to track her down, to get consent to reveal her whereabouts to her long lost daughter. All that the girl had to go on was her mother's name, which was Linda Watkins, and that she had been 16 years old at the time of her birth. Sandra had been adopted very soon after this and was brought up by her new parents in a village a few miles away. Seemingly this had been a very happy arrangement, but unfortunately her adoptive mother had died recently; obviously causing much sadness. And probably prompting Sandra's search for her birth mother.

Madame Zoe adjusted her turban and creamed her hands with shea butter; one of her little indulgences. When you are holding the hands of others, in an attempt to read their futures, it was important that your own looked their best. Sandra had booked a half-hour appointment. This length of time warranted the assistance of the crystal ball, currently residing on its gold trestle beneath a blue silk square.

What the client would not be able to see however, was the discreet screen resting on Madame Zoe's knees, with all the relevant information that she needed to provide a satisfying and remarkable experience for this young woman.

At the tinkle of the bell over the inner door, Marjorie, who had been wafting incense across the waiting room, crossed over to Sandra and offered her hand. The girl stood and looked around nervously, as if about to bolt for the street door, but at Marjorie's insistence she followed her through into the inner sanctum. There she was invited to take the chair across from Madame Zoe, whose hands stretched across the blue velvet cloth, palms upward in welcome.

'Hello my dear,' the gentle and soothing tones caused Sandra to straighten up in her chair. Zoe extended her well-buttered hand; taking the girl's thin and cold palm in hers.

'I understand that you seek some answers to very important questions today, but I would like to spend a few minutes sharing the thoughts and feelings that I am receiving from you.' She paused for effect and waited for the girl to respond.

'Okay, if you feel that is what we should do first,' Sandra was visibly shaking, and for just a moment, the fortune teller felt a smidgeon of remorse for the scam she was pulling. But business was business and she had her reputation for accuracy to uphold.

'My dear, I feel that you are going through a difficult time in your love life, and I see the letter S seems to be on your mind. Do you know someone with a name that begins with S?'

Sandra gasped and nodded her head in bemused agreement.

'Sadly, I feel that this person has behaved very badly, and that the relationship has come to an end. Would I be right about that?'

Again the girl nodded and Zoe smiled sweetly as she stroked the back of her hand.

For a moment or two Madame Zoe stared intently into Sandra's palm and then groaned theatrically.

'Ah, yes I see that you have been betrayed by a friend whose name begins with a J… No wait… I am wrong it is a T.

There was a satisfying gasp at the mention of the letter T and it was clear that there was another relationship that was over.

'I also feel that you work in a place that might be involved in legal matters,' she held up one finger of her free hand to prevent any interruption.

'Perhaps a police station, no don't tell me… I think it might be a solicitor's office, am I correct?'

By this time Sandra was hooked and it was now time to reveal the most important element of today's reading.

Claiming back her hand from the girl, Zoe lifted the blue silk square to unveil the glass orb beneath. Sandra's eyes were riveted on this piece of fortune telling magic that she had been told about by some of her girlfriends. They had assured her that Madame Zoe seemed to have a window into their lives and had seen many things that they had only confided in to friends. They had assured her they always left their appointments safe in the knowledge that love would find them, and fortune was theirs for the taking.

After a few minutes of silence as Madame Zoe sought to pad out the half hour, she raised a solemn face to stare into the wide-eyed Sandra's face.

Now confident that she had the girls complete attention, she delivered her next question in a fateful tone.

'My dear child, I sense that you seek another, who is not a man but a family member long lost to you.' You could have heard a pin drop. She continued.

'There is someone from your past that you have barely met, but you are desperate to reconnect to.' Both of her hands cradled the crystal ball in front of her as she searched its depths.

'You look for your mother.' With that Sandra clasped a hand over her mouth; tears filling her eyes. Absolutely stunned she stared at the exotic creature in front of her.

'I have her name on the tip of my tongue… Now let me see it begins with an L…Yes that's right, her name is Linda, is that correct my dear? Sandra nodded eagerly and waited with bated breath for the next pronouncement.

'I see that this woman has changed her surname more than once, and I see her living in Manchester, in a house with the number 15.'

With this Madame Zoe appeared to go into a trance. Sandra looked on in concern as she desperately waited for the woman to resume her revelations. She was about to interrupt, but Zoe raised her hand in a gesture to remain silent.

Sandra couldn't see that the mystic in front of her was consulting her hidden screen; waiting while Marjorie typed further information into the computer behind the reception desk.

Finally the silence was broken and with a smile of relief, Madame Zoe announced with a flourish.

'Your mother's surname is Baxter and she is looking forward to meeting you very much.' With that she collapsed against the back of the chair, and smiling weakly at her now very emotional client, waved her away from the table.

Sandra didn't know whether to hug or kiss this strange looking, all-seeing woman, but sensing that it would be unwelcome, she retreated through the door into the reception area. Marjorie was waiting behind the desk and while Sandra wiped her eyes and composed herself, the assistant prepared the bill for this momentous session.

Without looking at the cost, which was nearly a week's wages, Sandra handed over her credit card and gratefully tapped in her pin number.

'Please thank Madame Zoe for me, she is amazing, and I will pass on her information to all my friends… Thank you, thank you.' With that the smiling girl opened the door to the shop and headed off into her future.

After making sure that Sandra had gone, Marjorie locked the door and put the closed sign up for lunch and headed back into the consulting room. There she found Zoe divested of both turban and wig with her feet up on one of the velvet chairs.

'Well done Marjorie… all that Facebook chit chat between her and her mates was gold dust, but that was a stroke of genius hacking into the adoption agency. What a coincidence that the girl's mother had been in touch after their letters finally reached her. The girl should get their message informing her of her mother's name and address tomorrow and that will really seal the deal.'

Marjorie put two plates down on the table and settled herself into the vacated client's chair. 'It will soon be time to

What's in a Name?

put our charges up Mum,' she smiled across the table as she helped herself to a ham and cheese sandwich.

'Once the word gets around on Facebook about this latest prediction we are going to be overrun... Tenerife here we come.'

'Her mother laughed and then shook her head... No... I don't think so pet. I see Hawaii in our futures.'

Bonus Story

The Village Square

The first story in a new collection
"The Village Square"
to be released in 2018.

The Village Square

St. Faith's church stood on the outskirts of the small Hampshire village of East Stanton. A place of worship had been sited on this mound for centuries and there was evidence that a church had been dedicated there before 700 AD. In the 12th century, the present building had been constructed lovingly by local builders and had been renovated, probably by the descendants of those same builders in the 14th and the 19th centuries.

The last changes to the building had been made in Victorian times and had taken ten years. The money for the project had been provided by the then Squire, Richard Cranford whose great grandson, Edward, was now the current lord of the manor. There had been Crandford's in East Stanton since the Middle Ages and the family had served the monarchs of the country well throughout the centuries. This service had resulted in gifts of estates in the surrounding countryside.

The years had eroded this massive holding, but the squire still owned the largest farm in the area, as well as a substantial number of cottages and buildings in and around East Stanton.

In the churchyard to the rear of the grounds lay the well-ordered graveyard. Even the oldest stones stood strongly and the paths and graves themselves were immaculately kept by the team of volunteer gardeners. The most famous son of East Stanton, after the squire, was a naval captain, Joseph Stephens who had served and died with Nelson at Trafalgar. Nearly 135 years later, his descendants still left flowers on his grave each

What's in a Name?

anniversary and Frederick Stephens, who owned the butcher's shop in the square, proudly displayed a portrait of his illustrious ancestor on the wall of his establishment.

On this Sunday morning in early September, the small church was packed and many looked to the front pew where Edward Cranford, his wife Celia and their three children Elisabeth, Amelia and Teddy bowed their heads in prayer. The congregation was so large that many of the men huddled silently at the rear of the church, hats in hand and heads bowed. As the hands of the clock in the bell tower moved slowly towards the hour, the silence in this holy place intensified.

Generations of young men from East Stanton had served at sea. Like many villages in Hampshire that lay close to Portsmouth, joining the Royal Navy was an adventure that attracted many a farm boy reluctant to follow his father onto the land or serve the squire. Not many of those that served their country in the navy were buried in the small graveyard and in many cases, there were no gravestones anywhere, simply burial at sea. Over the last three hundred years, the women of the village had become accustomed to grieving for their seafaring husbands and sons. This morning they were remembered, as several widows of the First World War stood together, hands clasping hands for comfort.

The vicar, John Hogg looked out at his congregation, and for a moment his eyes rested on his own family in the choir stalls. His wife Bess looked up from her prayers and she smiled encouragingly at him. She placed her arms around her two daughters, Veronica and Grace as they stood by her side and she breathed deeply as she watched her husband move from the side of the altar.

Normally the Sunday service began at 11:00 to allow for the congregation who were mainly from the farming community to complete their early morning milking and

What's in a Name?

other essential jobs. This morning however, the church had begun to fill up shortly after 10:00 as word of this morning's events filtered through the efficient grapevine maintained in the village itself and surrounding farms and cottages. By 10:30, the church had been full and John Hogg had decided that his parishioners obviously needed to be together on what could be a momentous day in history. He too had heard the announcement made by the BBC as he was finishing his breakfast. The country was on standby for a speech from the Prime Minister at 11:15 and everyone knew that following the events of the last two days, this speech was likely to change the lives of everyone in the country forever.

As the vicar watched his friends and family standing with heads bowed, he knew that they would be remembering another time. They had been promised that following the devastation of the First World War there would be lasting peace. That the sacrifice of so many would have achieved that peace for future generations. The monument in the centre of the village square was testament to that sacrifice and there was hardly a family in the village that had not lost a father, brother, son or husband to that assurance. He himself had served in the trenches and been wounded twice before returning home to take holy orders. His two brothers had not been so fortunate and somewhere in a cemetery in Northern France, simple crosses marked their graves.

John had brought their wireless from the vicarage and he now placed it on a table in the centre of the aisle and switched the set on. At first, there was just hissing and static and then as the church clock struck 11:15, a voice could be heard clearly, filling the building with chilling clarity.

The solemn tone of their Prime Minister conveyed the dreaded message as eloquently as the words themselves. There was a sharp intake of breath from the assembled villagers as

What's in a Name?

Neville Chamberlain completed his sombre address. For a few short minutes hope had flared but then died. They had been promised that the last conflict had been 'the war to end all wars' and those words echoed in the congregations minds as they contemplated the future.

A cry fractured the silence and a woman collapsed against her neighbour and began to sob uncontrollably. Within minutes, the whole congregation was hugging and talking. Women cried on their husband's shoulders and mother's clasped embarrassed sons in their arms, desperately trying to hold onto them and keep them from harm.

The news was not unexpected. Since early 1937, the country had been preparing for war, and it was generally understood that a conflict with Germany was a certainty. Men from the First World War who were in the reserves or those serving in the Territorial Army had been mobilised.

Conscription had been abandoned after the First World War but by 1939, there were only around 200,000 soldiers in the British Army. It was painfully evident that there were not going to be enough men to take on the might of the German forces and earlier in the year, the Government had introduced the Military Training Act. This act meant that all men between the ages of 20 and 21 years old had to register for six months military training. Some occupations were classified as 'reserved' and essential to the war effort, and many a mother in the congregation was grateful that farmers and their workers were exempt. There had been talk of conscription being introduced for all men between the ages of 18 and 41 who were not in reserved occupations. Those boys who were eligible to be drafted and some older men looked at each other in silence.

At the back of the church, stood a group of men in their fifties and sixties, many of whom had served in the First War.

What's in a Name?

They had already formed into groups of Special Constables and Air Raid Wardens, trained and ready to deal with a very new type of warfare that would be waged in the skies and in bombing raids.

There was no doubt in all the villagers' minds that every single one of them would be affected in some way by the finality of the news today.

The vicar moved amongst the men, women and bewildered children, trying to give comfort but fighting his own feelings of fear and dismay. He felt guilty as he gave thanks for having no sons, only two daughters, but knew that many of the young men standing with their families today would not be here when and if peace was declared. He took a deep breath and moved out of the dark and cool church into the sunshine. The squire and his family followed him down the aisle and stood with him as he shook each hand that was outstretched towards him.

Edward Cranford had served in the Army Flying Corps in the First World War and was no stranger to fear and violence. Like John, he knew what was ahead but as he clasped the hands of the young men of the village, he could see in them the fire and desire to serve that he and his many dead comrades had felt when war had been declared in 1914. His son, Teddy, was 18 years old and was already planning on a career in the army. He shuddered as he fought back the feelings of panic and knew that the die was now cast.

By the time the last parishioner had left the small church, John felt exhausted. He was aware that his job would now change from a peacetime role as vicar of a country church to comforter and bearer of bad news. As the young men clustered together and talked excitedly, he wondered how many of their parents he would be visiting over the coming months and years to bring solace and faith.

What's in a Name?

He felt a hand slip into his own and looked down to the blonde head resting on his shoulder.

'John, let's go home please, I need to be with just you and the girls right now.'

Bess had lost a brother at the Somme and they had met when John had visited her parents after the war. He had served with Peter and been with him when he was killed and this had brought a bittersweet essence to the early days of their romance.

Their daughters Veronica and Grace were eighteen and nineteen and knew all the local boys from the various Saturday night dances held in the tennis, football and cricket clubs. There had been no serious romances but he could see from their pinched faces that they were afraid and upset. He put his arms around their shoulders and smiled at Bess.

'Come on darling, let's get these girls home and get lunch on. We can sit in the garden and talk about what is going to happen and how we can all help our friends in the village get through this next few days and weeks.'

The two girls smiled at their father and hugged him closer. They were bright girls and had questioned him ceaselessly about his time in the army, fascinated by his scars and eager to find something noble in what they had initially felt was one huge adventure. John had told them of that time without glorifying his role and over time, they came to understand the pain of both their father and mother's losses.

However, their mother knew that her daughters were not immune to the glamour of seeing their childhood friends in uniform and suspected that for the younger generation of the village, the horrors and devastation of war would be tempered with excitement for the opportunities it could offer.

As the family walked around the side of the church and through the graveyard, Bess reflected on the number

What's in a Name?

of young men who had left East Stanton for the army and navy and who had never returned. She thought about all the young men who had been at the service this morning and felt incredible sorrow for the life that they would now choose out of honour and loyalty to their country. Please God it would be over quickly and that they would all return home safe.

The squire and his family climbed into their car and drove up the hill, past the mill and through the square. Their house faced the war memorial and Edward slowed as the car drove past. Two of his cousins and his older brother's name were inscribed on the monument and he could recite all the names on the list by heart. These were his people and his responsibility. He was too old to serve in the armed forces now. But he would do whatever he could to protect both the village and its inhabitants from as much hardship as possible. There was no point in sitting around waiting for anyone in authority to do something, as they would have their hands full dealing with the enormity of the broader picture.

As he manoeuvred the car into the drive at the side of the house, he made a mental note of the people he would need to get together to put plans into action. Apart from the Special Constables and Air Raid Wardens he would need to speak to all the shopkeepers, the doctor and matron of the local nursing home to ensure that they were ready for whatever events took place including preparing for food shortages.

He glanced over his shoulder at his son Teddy in the back seat who smiled back at his father. He appeared to have gone from a boy to a man in the time it had taken the Prime Minister to make his fateful announcement. His two daughters looked tearful and both held their brother's hands tightly on their laps as if to keep him close.

In the homes and farms of East Stanton, the normally jovial Sunday lunches were subdued. Parlours were opened up and families came together from around the county to talk about the news and draw comfort from each other throughout the summer afternoon.

In the distance, the St. Faith's church bells rang out for evening service and as one, the villagers returned to their place of worship to face the uncertain future together.

The End

Acknowledgements

David Cronin for all the time spent in editing, formatting and designing my books. One in a million.

About the Author

Sally Cronin spent a number of years in each of the following industries – Retail, Advertising and Telecommunications, Radio & Television; and has taken a great deal of inspiration from each.

She has written short stories and poetry since a very young age and contributed to media in the UK and Spain. In 1996 Sally began studying nutrition to inspire her to lose 150 lbs and her first book, Size Matters published in 2001, told the story of that journey back to health. This was followed by another eight books across a number of genres including health, humour and romance.

For the last four years Sally has written a daily blog covering the subjects close to her heart and it is called **Smorgasbord Invitation – Variety is the Spice of Life**. You can link to it from here smorgasbordinvitation.wordpress.com

Sally Cronin

Your feedback would be appreciated.

*T*hank you for reading my book and it would mean a great deal to me if you could give me your opinion. Not only will this let me know what you feel about my writing in general, but potential readers will also value your feedback.

If you have bought this book from Amazon you will already have an account that will enable you to review books that you have bought, or have been given as a gift. If you have not bought the book yourself please mention that at the front end of the review so that it will be published. https://www.amazon.com

Goodreads *is an excellent site for readers and you can sign in with facebook or sign up with an email address. This gives you access to thousands of books, enables you to connect with readers of the genres you enjoy and leave reviews on any books that you have read and feel you would like to offer constructive comments.* https://www.goodreads.com/

Finally I would be delighted to hear from you by email about the book. (sally.cronin@moyhill.com)

You can link to this book through my author page on Amazon in the US and the UK.

Amazon USA:
http://www.amazon.com/Sally-Cronin/e/B0096REZM2

Amazon UK:
http://www.amazon.co.uk/Sally-Georgina-Cronin/e/B003B7O0T6

What will really help me in my future writing is to know some of the following in your review.

1. *What did you like or dislike about the style of writing?*
2. *What did you enjoy about the plots of the stories or of the novel?*
3. *How did you feel about the main characters and were they believable?*
4. *Was there a particular story in a collection or episode in the novel that you specifically enjoyed.*
5. *What were your feelings when you finished the book? Were you satisfied, wanted more or unsatisfied?*
6. *Is there anything else that you feel it is important to mention for the benefit of other readers*
7. *Did you like the cover and how the book was laid out inside? Was it easy to read?*
8. *Would you recommend the book to others?*

N.B. I appreciate that you may not feel comfortable in leaving your own name on a review, especially if you need to offer constructive criticism. I suggest that if you read a lot of books that you create your own pen name for your reviews. It can be as simple as "Avid Reader" or another fictional name. That way your identity is private.

Thank you very much for taking the time to let me know your opinion.

Best wishes
Sally Cronin

Just an
Odd Job Girl
Sally Georgina Cronin

Size
Matters
... Especially if you weigh 330 lbs!
Sally Georgina
Cronin

JUST
FOOD
for
Health
The common sense guide to the human body and the foods you need to eat to keep it healthy
Sally Georgina Cronin

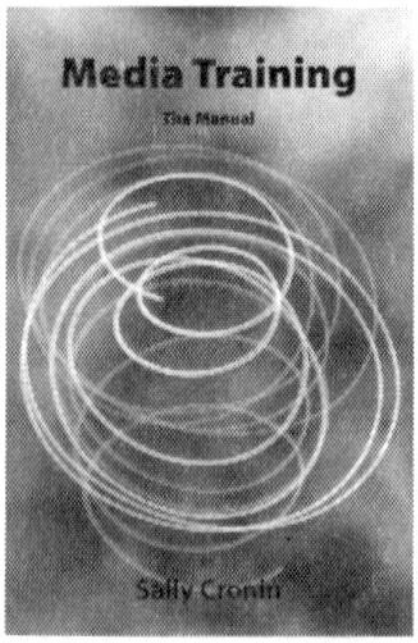
Media Training
The Manual
Sally Cronin

Sam
A Shaggy Dog Story
Sally Cronin

Your body is your greatest asset!
Are you getting the performance
you would like from it?
Forget the
VIAGRA...
Pass me a
CARROT!
Sally Cronin

Turning Back
the
Clock
How to feel and look
10 years younger
Sally Cronin

Flights
of Fancy
Sally Cronin

TALES FROM THE
GARDEN
Sally Cronin

What's
in a
Name?
Colourful Tales
by
Sally Cronin

WHAT'S
IN A NAME?
Stories of Life
and Romance
Volume 2
Sally Cronin